After

the

Storm

SEPIA BOOKS are published by

BET Publications, LLC
c/o BET BOOKS
One BET Plaza
1900 W Place NE
Washington, DC 20018—1211

All Kensington Titles, Imprints and Distributed Lines are available at special quantity discounts for bulk purchases for sales promotions, premiums, fund-raising, and educational or institutional use. Special book excerpts or customized printings can also be created to fit specific needs. For details, write or phone the office of the Kensington Special Sales Manager: Attn. Special Sales Department, Kensington Publishing Corp., 850 Third Avenue, New York, NY 10022, Phone: 1-800-221-2647.

ISBN: 1-58314-482-X

First Printing: June 2005
10 9 8 7 6 5 4 3 2 1

Printed in the United States of America

After the Storm

CASSANDRA DARDEN BELL

sepia

BET BOOKS

BET Publications, LLC
www.bet.com

Dedicated to my mother
Lillie Gorham Darden

Acknowledgments

To my editor, Glenda Howard, for guidance I can always trust. The fine folks at BET Books, VP Linda Gill, Publicity Director Kicheko Driggins, and Guy Chapman. The hardest working agent in the business, Sha Shana Crichton, for going the extra mile time and time again. My personal Publicity Director, Larry Bell, for adding class and quality to all that I do. Dee Pappas and the National Breast Cancer Coalition for providing research material and allowing me to tag along for Lobby Day 2002. Dr. Seodial Deena, East Carolina University, Rev. Eve Rogers, Laura Hamilton, Starling and Frances Bell, the Gershwins, and the many book clubs and bookstore managers who have been so gracious with your support of *Mississippi Blues*. To all of my family members who provided a warm bed and a hot meal while I was touring in your city . . . Elton and Diana Brown, David and Mia Shackleford, Walter and Velma Gorham, Sarah Smith, James and Monyetta Austin, Gaynell Moye, Joyce Gorham and Tamesha Bell. To my children—Lauryn, Ariel and Jordan—for being so patient when mommy is traveling, writing more books, and otherwise distracted.

1

____

May 20th, 2005

Paying off debt can easily be described as "better than sex."
And the larger the debt, the better the sensation. My mind is all
over the place as I fall into one of three lines forming at the
front counter of Southeast Bank. On most days, the sight of the
three old men and the woman pushing the baby stroller in front
of me would have put a sour note on my day. That combination
can turn a five-minute bank transaction into thirty minutes of
pure hell. The old men shamelessly flirt and gawk at the teller's
cleavage, as they cash their social security checks; and the woman
with the baby has to stop at least three times in the middle of her
transaction to quiet the tot. But this day, neither of those an-
noyances is going to ruin my mood.

"Is someone helping you?"

I spin around only to see the top of her strawberry blonde
hair. A short, round woman, wearing a navy blue business suit
whose double-breast jacket buttons are stretching the buttonholes out of proportion, gazes at me with professional concern.
I catch myself giving her the once-over before answering.

"Yes, I need to see someone about paying off a loan and
making a, well, a rather large deposit," I whisper, only wishing

I could jump onto one of the deposit-slip islands in the middle of the bank and yell it for all to hear.

"For the first time in my life, I have a large deposit and I'm paying off my loan early," I would say.

But that would have been inappropriate, so I simply follow the oval-shaped woman to an office clearly marked "Customer Service." I notice her tight calf muscles rippling with each step in her blue high-heel pumps. Her arm extends toward the door as her chubby hand guides me into the office.

"Someone will be right with you," she whispers, as I slide past her through the door.

She smiles pleasantly and wobbles off to pounce on the next unsuspecting person to walk through the revolving doors at the front of the bank.

I had been in the customer service office too many times when I first started my business. Either begging or almost begging for loans or extensions to already existing loans. But not this time. This time, I am in the driver's seat.

As I carefully plant my nervous behind into the leather seat, I notice the office looks abandoned. No generic ocean prints on the wall. No framed pictures of the kids or the family pet. Not even a pen or coffee mug to clearly say *someone had been here and would be back*.

Before I can get up to find out if I have been put in the holding cell until the powers that be decide to attend to me, he walks in. Dressed in an impressive black single-breasted suit with a white shirt and snazzy print tie. Clean-shaven and smelling good, 6'2" hunk of man that makes me forget my manners. His bald head is as smooth as a baby's behind and has a nice shine to it. His deep chocolate complexion looks like the part he didn't get through inheritance, but instead, most definitely came from long hours in the sun. It makes me think of a Snickers bar. The new kind with almonds instead of peanuts. I catch myself licking my lips as he maneuvers around the office.

"I'm sorry you had to wait. I'm Ty Basnight. Ty, short for Tyrese, just moved to town from Raleigh, North Carolina, at your service," he says, as he drops a pile of papers on the desk and extends his hand toward mine.

I stand up, not sure what else to do, and introduce myself.

"Jessica Andrews, nice to meet you," I say, reaching for his outstretched hand.

A rather rugged hand for a man in a suit, working in an office. At first sight his nails look manicured, but on closer inspection the small calluses at the base of his fingers tell a different story. Perhaps from gardening or weight lifting, I think, as I start to tell him about my banking needs. But Ty Basnight is too far into his "all about me" speech. So I sit back down and listen as he fumbles with the computer and the pile of papers strewn in front of him. His accent sounds like a cross between Andy Griffith and intelligent, articulate blacks in the presence of equally intelligent white folk. Big words with just a hint of southern drawl. I'm not sure of what he said because my mind is on the little red button on the side of the desktop computer. The tiny red button to give the surge of power Ty is obviously searching for with no luck. After running his hand around the entire perimeter of the machine, he finally comes across the button, flips it and keeps running his mouth.

"Yeah, moved to town just about a week ago. Still trying to figure out which one of those bridges leads to my apartment."

I giggle politely, acknowledging the bridge problem. I've been in Jacksonville, Florida, all my life, and if my mind isn't on it, I still take the wrong bridge. But I can't tell Mr. Basnight that because he is still yapping and fooling with the computer.

I assume his nervousness is the cause of his rambling, so I sink comfortably in my seat and watch him fumble with papers, waiting for the electronic dinosaur that has seen better days to power up and show some sign of intelligent megahertz. Since Mr. Basnight is in his own world, and I am somewhat the computer geek, I give the computer a good once-over. The machine is a Pentium 166 and, to make matters worse, they are using Windows NT. Although that means nothing to most people, I find it amusing for a bank of this size.

Ty Basnight is deeper into his life story waiting for something to pop up on the screen. Finally, a log-in screen comes up and I almost laugh out loud. I know something Ty obviously does not. For whatever reason, the bank is running NT on a Novell network and no one has bothered to give Ty the password. I inwardly hate myself for letting this technological beast take my attention off the handsome specimen in front of me. Ty Basnight is quick on his feet, discovers the problem, and casually moves his hands from the keyboard back to those same papers he was tossing around when he came in.

He is gorgeous, with polished white teeth that shine brighter against his dark skin. A mouth full of teeth that I might have time to count if he continues his rambling. He finally makes eye contact with me after a few of the papers slide off the front of the desk and land at my feet. We both burst out laughing at the "first impression from hell."

I pull my papers from the burgundy portfolio and slide them across the desk.

"I think this is what you're looking for."

His eyes lock on mine with a glare that makes me feel the heat rising from under my blouse. He continues smiling as he rubs his hand across his damp forehead. The motion makes me want to do the same as I wonder if someone has secretly turned the heat on in this office.

"I must look like an idiot. They told me to come in and help you, handed me these papers that I assumed had something to do with why you're here, but anyway, I'm sorry, Mrs. Andrews."

"No problem. And it's Ms.," I add, not moving my eyes from his. "This was quite entertaining. You shuffle papers and bullshit very well for so early in the morning." I giggle again, knowing full well I'm flirting with Mr. Basnight and his absolutely bare left ring finger.

I assume, being a country boy, Ty does not catch my worldly sophisticated technique, but he catches it just fine.

"Well, you'll have to let me make it up to you, Ms. Andrews," he adds with an equally flirtatious tone.

Ty Basnight takes the papers, reads over them, and leaves the room to get the ball rolling on my payoff. He is in and out of the office, asking questions about the type of loan and payoff penalties, and adding the occasional compliment that is raising Ty's score on the date potential card.

I get up from the seat in his makeshift office and look out the door, hoping to see him coming with the final papers for me to sign. Instead, he is scurrying around with one of the tellers, looking into files and printing things from the main computer. He throws up his index finger indicating he will be with me in just a minute. As he and the slim teller in a flower-print dress walk off, I know I have many minutes to wait, and for the first time in a long time, I don't mind.

During Ty's absence, I have too much time to think. Not about my successful business, the huge check I just handed him, or the thirty pounds I lost during the past year. Instead, my mind drifts back to what was clearly the worst day of my life. The day I walked into Happy Motors Used Car Dealership and found my husband stretched out on the floor, grunting and squirming between the legs of Minnie, his new auto parts girl.

2

August 28th, 2002

I woke up with a sinking feeling in the pit of my stomach. After getting my shower and first cup of coffee, I realized the feeling wasn't the result of something I had eaten the night before. It was more internal; either my heart or my head wasn't clicking in time with things around me. My twin boys, Joshua and Jared, thought I had lost my mind. Eight-year-old boys rarely think their mother is all there, but they seemed a little more leery of me on that morning. I half answered most of their questions, let them wear whatever they wanted to school, and wouldn't let them turn on the television set. And that is sheer anguish for young boys who need their daily fill of Nickelodeon. After watching me scamper around all morning, they seemed relieved when the school bus pulled up in front of the house, and they were rescued from the quiet chaos.

I had had that uneasy feeling before, and it has never been a sign of anything good. If it did mean there was life-altering information coming my way, I didn't want to find out on television or radio, so I wouldn't listen to either. I've always had this fear of hearing about the death of a loved one while watching some cold, lifeless news report: "Officials say there were no survivors and they are still investigating the cause of the accident . . ." [awkward pause] ". . . and now Brett takes a look at that weekend forecast." No one wants to hear about death through a news report and certainly not from a reporter who obviously failed Segue Class.

After the boys were gone, with one cup of coffee, two twelve-ounce cans of Diet Coke, and one stale chocolate-covered donut under my protruding Gucci belt, I made up my mind to get out of the house despite the pestering uncertainty in my gut. No sooner than I grabbed my newest Coach handbag and opened the front door, it hit me. The muggy warmth of hurricane season.

It's a damp stillness that hangs in the air. The low, fast-moving clouds and uneasiness of the wind pushing against the palm trees speak to you. There's almost a smell attached to it. You see locals walk out, look up, sniff the air, and put their hands on their hips only to announce, "Feels like a storm coming, hope it isn't a bad one."

Even in northern Florida, hurricane season means keeping your head up and your eyes open. Before you have time to react to the feeling, the wind and rain could toss your world into utter chaos, leaving only a mangled mess and victims surveying what's left with tears in their eyes and their mouths dropped open. No matter how many times the storms have blown through, you're never quite ready for it. The weather reports, the home and garden chains selling wood pallets, even the empty grocery shelves: nothing ever prepares you for what Mother Nature can do on a day with a feeling and a smell like this.

Assured that my nagging was simply a sign of a storm brewing, I ran back inside, grabbed the remote, and hit the power button. Sure enough, meteorologist Skip Meadows was spouting off the latest about a change in the path of the storm and giving the coordinates of Hurricane Lily. He was warning Floridians from the tip to the top to get ready for the high winds and heavy rains. I hit the power button again, killing Skippy in mid-sentence, knowing I'd have less time to get all my errands run before the boys were sent back home from school early, and Lily shut life down for a few hours or even days.

Having wasted too much time worrying about some unexpected mishap, I grabbed the purse again, tossed it over my right shoulder. A quick glance at the wrist watch revealed that the ten o'clock hour was approaching at an alarming pace, so I grabbed an umbrella and dashed to my car. With my mind on at least four things at one time, I started the engine, put the car in gear and started backing out of the driveway without looking. A quick glance in the rearview mirror just as I reached for my cell phone sent chills up and down my spine. The mailman with his mouth and eyes open wide was standing carelessly at the end of my driveway trying to shove past-due bills into the box. I slammed the brakes and screamed as my heart pounded against my chest cavity. Mr. Mailman scooted his narrow rear just out of reach of my left bumper.

I rolled down my window to make sure he was okay, as he threw up a forgiving wave, kept shoving mail, and then moved to the other side of the street to avoid the horrible death by motor vehicle I almost inflicted. After he was clearly out of the way, I pulled out of the driveway, trying to stay calm enough to make the call to my husband, Derrick.

"Happy Motors, Carol speaking, how may I direct your call?"

"Hey Carol, this is Jessi."

"Oh, hey girl, what'cha up to?" she added, relaxing her tone.

"Nothing much, just looking for Derrick. Is he free?"

"Probably not. Said he was working on something important," she offered, smacking gum in my ear.

"I'm trying to get a few errands in this morning. I think he picked up my checkbook, so now I've gotta come over there before I can get my stuff done."

"You know there's a storm, don't you?" she said, letting the gum smacking subside momentarily.

"Yeah girl, but if I don't get this stuff done now, there's no telling when. Might be a good time since everybody else will be at the grocery store getting milk and bread."

"Know what you mean, I'm on my way there too. Bye now," she giggled, popped her gum, and hung up.

Derrick owned a used-car business. Although he'd taken his share of ribbing over the years with all the used-car-salesman jokes, he really didn't fit the bill, and I never could figure out why he didn't try his hand at something else. He had opened the shop less than six months after we were married on a dare from one of his poker buddies. After too many beers, and one too many conversations about how slick he was, they convinced him that he could sell condoms to a nun, and thus Happy Motors Used Cars was born.

The annoying feeling I had woken up with had taken on a more physical nature by the time I drove the two blocks along Atlantic to the shop. I attributed it to my nutritious breakfast as I thought about how nice it must be for Derrick to work only a couple of blocks from our house. The drive to the shop was no more than five minutes on a normal day, but with the storm brewing, the working commuters were not the only ones on the roads. Old folks eager to raid the bread aisle were puttering along at thirty-five miles per hour in zones clearly marked forty-five. I tried not to be impatient as I approached the first stop-light, which almost immediately turned green. I slammed my foot back down on the accelerator and pulled off trying to maneuver my way into the right lane. I finally got a clearing to pass an old man with a few strands of white hair on his speckled head. I laughed as my car lined up beside his. He didn't look my way, but it was clear he knew I was there when his knuckles almost bulged through the skin under his tightened grip. I passed him and continued dodging in and out of traffic.

As I pulled into the driveway of the car lot, I noticed that Carol's car was gone. She would likely be dragging her wide behind down the same aisle with the frail white-haired man I had just passed. I didn't have much room to talk when it came to rear ends, but Carol has the kind of booty that looks like a hump on her lower back. Her posture doesn't help the hump effect either, since her size double Ds made her lean forward like she was about to tip over. I could just see her wobbling down that grocery-store aisle, butt in the air, head stuck forward with reading glasses dangling off the end of her nose, grabbing the last two loaves of Nature's Own Honey Wheat.

I drove up the back lot, the lot that led directly to Derrick and Carol's office. There were plenty of other cars parked in the employee lot. The service guys, all led by chief mechanic Drew Stanley, and of course the auto parts girl Minnie. Minnie's little Mazda Miata was parked right in front of the door, almost blocking the entrance. But my attention got glued to Drew Stanley's old beat-up Ford pickup truck. That Ford pickup had spent more time in the repair shop, or alongside the road, than in good working order. You'd think a mechanic could keep his own vehicle working, but Drew always joked that it got him where he needed to go. Would've been closer to the truth to say it almost got him where he needed to go. My humorous thoughts of Drew and his vehicle problems were interrupted by the ringing inside my handbag.

"We're home, Ma," the voice shouted at me with rap music blaring in the background.

Just as I suspected, the boys were out of school and ready to anchor down for the storm. My day of errands was officially ruined. Like any responsible mother, I would get my checkbook from Derrick and join the other shoppers to get what was left of the nonperishable items from the grocery shelves.

"Sounds like a waste of time to me. Why did they even have school today," I shouted back, hoping my voice would punch through the music.

"They said as long as we're there until eleven o'clock, then it counts as a whole day," Josh chimed with the details. "But we were there just long enough for Jared to have his vocabulary test," he teased, and I could hear Jared whining in the background.

"Stay inside, and turn that music down. I'll be along as soon as I get a few things from the store."

"Cocoa Puffs and lots of chips, Ma. Please, we might be here for days," Josh insisted, as Jared yelled his request for ice cream.

I hit the end button before the list grew. My mind now shifted into storm mode. When I jumped out of the car, the warmth was still there even though the wind had picked up. I twirled my keys around my middle finger and shut the car door, imagining an evening at home refereeing shouting matches between the monotonous weather reports—that is, until Lily shut down all power. I made a mental note of the things I needed to pick up if we got shut down for a few days, still smiling to myself, as I added the boys' requests to the other responsible items.

The door to the office area was locked, so I trotted around to the front of the shop and went into the customer entrance. It was always open. I walked the long hall past the unoccupied parts counter, assuming Minnie was in the restroom applying more blood-red lipstick. I kept on past Derrick's office, peeking in only briefly to see his briefcase and keys still on the desk. I kept walking, casually bopping my head to the song that was playing ahead in the break room. Barry White was bellowing out the sensual lyrics of "Secret Garden," when I turned down the hall and up the four steps that led to the tiny room that doubled as Derrick's private break room and staff meeting room. I slid the door open hoping not to disturb Derrick if he was in the middle of something. That was my routine whenever I visited him at work. Pop my head in, get his acknowledging bow, and then wait for him to finish and join me in the hall. That was the plan this time, but when I peeked in, there were no clients sipping Coke, or salesmen and mechanics chumming it up with the boss. There was Derrick on the floor between the refrigerator and the table, with his shirt still on, his pants down around his knees, and his round brown butt moving up and down between two light brown, perfectly shaven legs.

I screamed, but no sound came out. The Barry White song was ending and the melody slowly fading as the grunting and panting got louder. Derrick's hips thrust up and down, while a tiny light brown butt lifted from the floor to meet his pressure, his force, and his movements. Her tan rayon skirt was clearly up around her waist as she moaned and dug her nails into his back almost ripping the starched white shirt I had picked up from the cleaners the day before. Derrick's right hand was supporting his weight as his left hand moved up and down, cupping her breasts, and almost breaking the buttons on her red blouse. The music faded, and I was sure they would hear me gagging from the doorway, but they were both in another place as he moaned, clamping his eyes shut tight and twisting his mouth to the left and right and scrunching his face as if in pain.

"Oh Minnie," he growled as his thrust quickened.

He grabbed on to one of the legs of the table to steady himself. I tried to look away, but hearing her name kept my eyes glued to the awful sight. It was that little slut he had just hired even though she had no employable skills.

She cried out, "Oh God, Jesus . . . Jesus," as her head flew back and her mouth gaped wide open as if gasping for air.

I thought the table was going to fall over on them as Derrick yanked it hard to give his lower body more leverage. I stumbled back out the door and down the four steps and bumped into Drew. He grabbed me and wanted to know what was wrong. I didn't want to break down in front of him. I didn't want Derrick and his parts lady to know I had seen them. I couldn't breathe. I put my hand around my neck to signal that I was choking; gasping for air, the same kind of gasping Minnie was doing just a few feet away.

"Mrs. Andrews, you all right?"

I couldn't answer Drew. His grease-covered hands reached toward me and I almost reached back to him, needing his strength to hold me up. Instead, I pulled away from him just before the tears started. I ran down the long hall wanting to get as far away as possible. Instead of going into the break room, Drew followed me, still reaching and beckoning. I stumbled out the same door I had just bounced through, knowing my life had been changed forever. Drew was right on my heels, chanting my name.

"I'll be fine," I yelled back as Drew picked up his pace and almost caught me.

I jumped into my car, revved the engine, and drove off, leaving Drew standing there with his arms outstretched. Leaving the Happy Motors used car lot for the last time ever.

3

The rain started as soon as I got into my car. The huge droplets were pounding from all sides as I drove along watching palm trees bend and shake under the force of the wind. Having been in Florida all my life, I knew this was only the beginning. By the time the hurricane made landfall, the wind and rain would be so strong it could move houses and cars. As strong as it felt whipping past me now, it was merely the equivalent of a strong thunderstorm, with the worst part just around the corner. The clouds tell the story. Darker, heavy-looking clouds were moving in, mixing with the wind, rain, and tears. It all made driving more dangerous, so I pulled over into the strip mall just down the street from the car lot, and attempted to dry my eyes enough to see my way clearly. But where was I trying to see my way to? There was no place to go. I couldn't go home. As soon as my mind toyed with the word *home*, I thought of the boys. I reached for my cell phone to call them, to assure them that I was on my way. But I couldn't assure anyone of anything. And a gagging sensation was forming at the base of my throat. There was too much happening at once. I used my shirtsleeve to dry my eyes, but they just felt wetter.

I opened the door and leaned out just in time to throw up pieces of chocolate donut and what tasted like the stinging burn of Coke the second time around. I watched the particles mingle with the rain on the roadside and slowly disappear, like I hadn't just tossed them there with violent force.

I closed the door and looked around to see if anyone might have seen the spectacle. My life had just fallen apart and I was concerned about someone seeing me. But who was there to see or care? I looked around to see only a few cars in the parking lot. The roads were clearing a little as most of the Floridians had gotten their supplies and gone home to batten down the hatches in preparation for Lily. There were still the stragglers, the ones who waited until the last minute to figure out they needed things for the storm. The men rushing into the Safeway for batteries and bottled water, and me, an emotional wreck rushing nowhere.

The windshield wiper blades scraped across the sheet of glass in front of me, clearing the way for only a second, and then the glass was blurred again. By the rain or my tears, I wasn't sure which. I wiped my eyes again with the already soaked shirtsleeve while yanking open the glove box to find tissue. After soaking several sheets, I reached deep within myself to gather enough strength to take care of the most immediate thing. The boys.

With fewer cars on the road, I was pulling up in my driveway in no time. As if my life hadn't just fallen apart, I sprung into action, scurrying around like a mother hen gathering her babies.

"Get a bag. Pack some things. We're going to Grandma's," I said, watching the two of them moving in slow motion, staring at me like they had seen a ghost.

As much as they loved going to Grandma's, it had to be a shock that we were paying a visit with a hurricane pounding on our door. I placed my hand on my hip and cocked my head to one side—my sign to them that I am serious. And they picked up the pace. Jared headed toward their bedroom while Josh circled me trying to figure out what was going on. As he passed in front of me, my eyes fell on the fresh haircut Derrick had just given him the night before. Tall for his age, I knew that before long he'd be able to look me eye to eye during the circling. But for now, he'd tilt his head upward each time he passed in front of me. His deep brown eyes beaming with a million questions.

"But there's a storm," Josh announced walking around me for the third time. "And where's Daddy?"

The question felt like a kick in the stomach. I tried not to wince. I didn't want to think where Daddy was. I didn't want to see the sight again. But the mere mention of his name brought it back. In color and darting through my heart like mental snapshots. I blinked it away.

"He's on his way. But I'm taking you guys to Mama's until the storm passes over. She needs two strong men to look out for her during this thing," I teased, rubbing my hand over his head.

The action warranted a smile and the questioning eyes brightened in anticipation of hanging out at Grandma's.

Jared came back into the room with a bag packed full. He lifted one arm, bent it upward and shoved the tiny muscle into my face. The gesture yielded a smile from me. And I wasn't sure where it came from, since my insides were still weeping.

I wanted to look inside the bag to see what he had stuffed inside to make it bulge so. But I didn't have the strength to argue and search for the things they needed. I figured they'd left enough underwear and t-shirts at mama's to get them through. Joshua looked at Jared's bag and proclaimed that it looked like enough for him too, so the packing was done.

With no time to spare, I rushed the boys into the car; we sped across town being shoved and whipped by wind and rain all the way. Other than a few last-minute shoppers and rescue personnel, most other traffic had cleared out. I had planned to call my mother to let her know I was going to drop the boys off. But then I would have to explain why. Words of explanation wouldn't form in my brain, so I just drove. If we were standing on her doorstep, drenched and desperate, she would have to take them in and get an explanation later.

The boys didn't talk during the drive. As much as I tried to act like what we were doing was normal, I knew their minds were questioning it. Just like the wind was pushing and pulling my car across the broken yellow lines of the road, their unspoken questions slammed around my head. Why was I taking them out in the storm, when they were perfectly safe and dry at home? And where was their father? What had happened? But unlike the storm, neither of them pushed. They never said a word, and for this I would always be grateful.

4

When I got to my mother's house, she was sitting in her living room in the dark, sipping tea. The lights were out because of the storm. Not because of power loss, but because Mama believed that the storm was God doing his work and any respectable person would stop all activity, and allow God his time. The boys rushed in, smothering her with hugs and the damp cold of outside. The surprise of the visit showed on her face, but she didn't verbalize it. She wouldn't. Not in front of the boys.

I looked around the room to keep my eyes from lingering on her for too long. Despite my best efforts to keep things from her, she was good at reading me. My expression gave me away, and this was one time I couldn't afford to have that happen. I wasn't ready to deal with anyone until I had a chance to sit still long enough to process what had happened.

She squirmed in her chair, and swiped at the beads of water on her red button-down blouse. Her starched blue jeans and white gym socks completed what we all had come to know as the hurricane ensemble. Mama always dressed for going to a shelter even though she'd never left her home during a storm, and never really had to. But she was always ready. Jeans and a casual shirt were made for spending days and nights with strangers in cramped shelters. I looked down beside the recliner where she was sitting and there was the duffle bag. Without inspecting, I knew the contents were more of what she was already wearing. Casual shelter wear. And her brand-new white tennis shoes sat beside the chair, in position, ready to receive her socked feet at a moment's notice. Although this was a sight I saw at least four or five times each fall during hurricane season, today it was all I could focus my attention on.

"Boys, go ahead and get out of those wet clothes. Let me talk to Granny for a minute," I said, searching for something to do with my hands.

I slid my index finger in and out of the key-ring hole and shifted my weight from one foot to the other. I saw my mother's eyes lingering on my hands, so I held the keys still and tried not to swallow too hard as tightening formed at the base of my throat. The boys looked back and forth from me to Mama as they left the room. She lifted her hand and shooed them off; her motion seemed to make their steps quicken. One thing for sure, she loved the boys and they loved her. This would be the perfect place for them to camp out while my world fell apart outside. As soon as Mama was sure the boys were out of earshot, she turned her attention back to me, indignation and query in her eyes.

"What is going on, Jessi?" she said, before I could get in my two cents' worth and get out.

"I just need to leave them here for now, that's all. Will that be a problem?"

"Leave them. Where are you going?"

"I don't know, but I just need for you to watch them for me. At least until the storm passes."

"It's a hurricane, Jessi. Not a thunderstorm. I don't mind the boys. You know that. Love the company, but you don't need to be out in this mess. And where is Derrick?" she added, looking behind me as if he should be walking through the door any minute.

"I can't talk about this now, Mama."

"Jessi, what have you done?" she continued badgering, without regard for a word I was saying.

"What have I done? That's your first thought. That I've done something. Because Derrick would never do anything wrong, right Mama? Because I'm the screw-up."

"I didn't say that. I just mean that you women today aren't willing to work through stuff. The least sign of trouble and you ready to pack up and go."

"Yeah, that's my problem, Mama. Not willing to stick it out. And I'm going to take marriage advice from you, of all people."

"You watch your mouth, girl. Don't sass me, and lower your voice. You gonna upset those boys."

"I need to go. I'll call you."

"Jessi, whatever it is, it can't be bad enough for you to be out in this mess," she said, to the back of my head. "Jessi," she yelled over and over as I rushed out the door.

I didn't turn to respond, just stumbled to my car in the pounding rain. My clothes were soaked, my body aching and my cell phone ringing by the time I got inside the car. I looked at the number of the incoming call. It was Derrick. I didn't answer. As much as I wanted to concentrate on how bad I hurt from what I had seen, now the pain of my mother only seeing the worst in me was competing with it. I think she fell in love with Derrick before I did, and even then, she thought the man could do no wrong. Whenever we'd had problems in the past, she was convinced that it was because I wasn't up to par. When she wasn't complaining about my poor cooking skills, it was the fact that I still hadn't lost all the weight from my pregnancy. She even said that if Derrick got a wandering eye, it was because I had let myself go. With too much to be depressed about, I couldn't let her words linger in my head. Besides, she had no room to talk, since Daddy left her so long ago most people don't even remember that she was married. I flipped on the windshield wipers as if their motion would help get her words out of my head. It didn't work, but I was desperate. I had to do something, go someplace. I couldn't go back inside, and I couldn't just sit in her driveway forever either. I saw her hand pulling back the living-room curtain several times. I knew that if I sat there any longer, she would come to the car and make my life more miserable. So, I started the engine and drove off. With my mind barely in focus, I drove to the only place that made sense to me. My best friend's house.

The storm tossed me around the road, but somehow the despair in my heart was heavier than the fear of the storm. Fortunately there were still a few other cars on the roads, so I used headlights and taillights to guide me. My subconscious must have kicked in and provided the directions because my mind was drifting back and forth, from Derrick to my mother to the boys. Before I knew it, I was pulling into the driveway. I turned the car off and just sat. I couldn't move, couldn't get out of the car. I felt all my senses slipping away from me. Exhaustion, fear, and anger were replacing rational thought. So, I called her on my cell phone. It was simple enough. I pressed the number sign and then one on the keypad. Speed dial immediately pulled up 555-2963, with the name listed below it, Karen St.Clair.

5

Karen has been my best friend since we were grade-schoolers. Her family moved into our neighborhood in Orange Park when we were just six years old. Karen's mom didn't work, her dad was a navy seaman stationed at Mayport, and her two older sisters were almost in high school when they moved to our neck of the woods.

From the beginning, Karen's dad was absent. The excuse was "military deployment." We found out later it was a polite form of separation that wasn't supposed to scar the kids like outright divorce. Parents should give kids a little more credit. Which scars worse, the absence or the lies? No matter, that's the way it was with Karen's parents—never called a spade a spade. Her mother just went on hoping her father would return and they could be one big happy family. That never happened.

When I called that day, her husband, Randy, answered the phone.

"Hello Randy, this is Jess. Is Karen there," I asked, sounding far too formal, but Randy didn't seem to notice.

Of course she was there. Karen was always there. With a husband, a two-year-old, and a newborn baby, there was no place else she wanted to be.

"Hey Jess, you sound like you're on your cell. You out in this storm?"

The last thing I wanted to do was small talk with Randy, but I didn't want to tip him off, so I politely continued with the banter until I could take no more.

"If Karen is busy, I could just call later."

"Oh no, she's right here. Got Justin hanging on one leg and Kayla on her breast," he laughed, as he finally handed the phone to Karen.

"Hey Jess, ignore Randy, he's just jealous because he's not the one on this breast. What's up?"

"I need to talk to you. I need to see you."

"Okay, well, it sounds important, but I'm a little tied up at the moment, and there's a little thing called a hurricane ripping it up outside," she giggled.

"It's Derrick. I caught him with someone."

"Oh God, Jessi," she yelled. And then I heard Randy in the background begging to know what was wrong.

"Karen, I'm sitting in my car in your driveway. I think I'm dying," was all that I could manage to say before the dam burst.

The rain and wind were whipping harder and I felt my car move with the intermittent gusts. I tossed the cell phone down on the passenger seat and grabbed the tissue box. I saw Karen's front door fly open as she tore out, still trying to get her shoes on. Randy was holding Kayla in his arms, trying to shield her from the whipping rain. As she reached for the handle to get into my car, I started clearing soggy tissue off the passenger seat. My cell phone rang and when I flipped it over, it was Derrick's cell number again. I hit the power button to stop the ringing.

Karen was standing in the rain fumbling with my door handle, not even bothering to cover her shoulder-length blonde hair, since it was already soggy and dripping on her dark blue raincoat. She shoved the useless umbrella under the left side of her open raincoat and yanked the door open. She was wearing a blue pair of Levi's and a black J. Crew t-shirt. I knew it was

J. Crew; all her t-shirts were. I noticed that her sockless feet were sporting a pair of black loafers as she threw her left leg into the car. Most women wouldn't bother to notice what kind of shoes a person is wearing after finding her husband having sex with another woman, but I'm into shoes. Shoes and handbags are my thing. I notice them without thinking.

Karen didn't bother to take off her coat or ask what happened, she simply threw her arms around me and pulled me close. I was glad she didn't ask because tears had choked back the words. I couldn't speak if I wanted to. Karen sat there holding me and rocking back and forth as if I were one of her children needing the loving arms of a parent. As I let my pain roll down my cheeks, I wondered how she got so good at this kind of thing. Some people just have a knack for being there and knowing how to be there. She knows when to speak and when to just let silence do the talking. I wondered if she ever needed someone to be there for her; then I remembered the first time Karen met it face to face. The thing black people almost accept as the norm. The first time Karen dealt head-on with racism.

It was eighth grade when Karen met Randy St. Clair. We were in biology class and as much as Karen and I tried to get seats beside each other, the seating chart would not allow it. I ended up beside the class geek, Ulysses Martin, and Karen got Randy. I don't know how the conversation started, but the two of them walked out of class together talking about the fact that both of them have that little chin dimple thingy. To the two of them they were just talking about facial features, but to the rest of us, we saw chemistry taking over biology class.

Within no time, Karen finally admitted having the hots for Randy and that's when the drama started. There were plenty of other mixed-race couples like Karen and Randy in our high school, but Karen's parents were not so open-minded about their budding puppy love. Having a military base in our back-yards meant having people from all backgrounds and national-ities. For most folk, meeting and dating people of different races was okay, but in Karen's house it was crossing the line.

Karen was able to hide her secret for a while, but before long her mom and sisters found out about Randy, and world war three broke out.

The incident even warranted an extended stay from Karen's dad, who was supposed to be at sea but managed to come home when he found out his baby girl was "lip locking a black boy," as he put it. Since Karen spent most of her time at my house, she had managed to see Randy for months and no one was the wiser. My parents thought he was there to see me, so it was the perfect cover, until Karen got careless and stayed out on the porch hugged up with Randy a few minutes too long. Her sister Carol had come over to get her and walked up on Karen and Randy in an anything-but-friendly embrace on my back porch. As much as Karen begged her sister not to tell, it had the reverse effect.

Karen was forbidden to see Randy. They went along with the program and pretended to end things during high school, but as soon as we all left for college, Karen let her parents know she would do what she wanted. The three of us got an apartment together and started college at Florida State University. Karen's parents played hardball at first and wrote her off. After a few months of missing her baby girl, Karen's mom started visiting us at college and giving Karen money. When her dad found out about it, that was the final blow to their lame excuse for a marriage. They divorced and went their separate ways for good. Karen's sisters took advantage of the divorce and played their dad against their mom to get what they wanted. Karen reacted differently and pulled closer to Randy and me. We became her immediate family.

In a matter of eleven years we had gone from six-year-old pesky little girls playing together to best friends to sisters in a way closer than blood could ever make you. So Karen was my obvious choice to talk about seeing my husband doing the unthinkable.

"Jess, I'm sorry. What happened, what did he do?"

"The girl at his job. The new one. I walked in on the two of them."

It was harder to verbalize than I thought it would be, even to my best friend who had been trying to tell me that Derrick was up to no good. For at least eight years she had been trying to tell me. And I had been telling myself it was just my imagination. Karen sat silently while I babbled through tears.

Karen wasn't judgmental of my situation, but I still felt ashamed just being in her presence. She's the kind with the perfect hair that falls into place as she steps out of the shower. Her size-six figure looks great in all the latest fashions and she's married to one of the hottest, most intelligent, most decent black men I know. That's right. Randy was fine then, but now he's downright sexy. Standing 6'2" and "cut up." He has a tiny mole just above the left corner of his mustache. His mother was part Chinese, so his eyes are kind of slanty which makes him look like he's flirting. And he treats Karen like her stuff is trimmed in gold.

For all practical purposes I should hate Karen. Her strength, her perfect family life with Randy, and a two-year-old son and two-month-old daughter. Randy is a pediatrician and she's a nurse who works a flex schedule so she can be at home with the kids. Only two months after having the baby, she's back in her size-six jeans and hitting the gym regularly. I wanted to hate her especially now since my world was so messed up. I wanted to toss her little perfect white behind out of my car and tell her what a slap in the face it is when they take our good black men. Why do they have to get the good ones? Why couldn't she get the one who had no more character than to screw a coworker right there on the job? Why couldn't I get the doctor and the two kids, and the damn half-million-dollar home in Queen's Harbor? I tried to hate her. Even as she tried to console me, I wanted to lash out, take my anger out on her, but I couldn't. It's hard to hate family, blood, and that's what Karen is to me, just like a blood sister.

"I can't go back there today; I can't deal with him right now. He called just as I drove up. I didn't answer."

Karen reached down and picked up the cell phone. She ran her hand over it, as if trying to imagine and feel what I was going through. The anguish of not knowing what to do next and the simple thought of a phone call being too much to handle.

"Where are the boys?"

"Mama's."

"What did you tell her?"

"I didn't tell her anything. But she knew something was wrong. Who abandons her kids in the middle of a hurricane?"

"Did she press you?"

"No, but she blamed me. As usual. So I just left. Came straight here."

The car rocked from side to side. The howling sound sent a chill up my spine. I grabbed my arms and hugged them tight to my body.

"Come inside, Jess."

"No, Randy and the kids are there. I'm a mess; you don't need me in the way."

"Have you lost your mind? You wouldn't be in the way, you're family, Jess. I insist. You're coming in."

"No, I need to be alone and give this some time to sink in and figure out what I'm going to do."

"You shouldn't be alone, not tonight. There's a storm and, besides, you just don't need to be by yourself. Call Regina."

"Regina," I yelled.

Just the thought of having to face her was more than I wanted to deal with, even in theory.

"She's probably not even in town and if she is, she doesn't have time to babysit me for the night. She's probably at Reginald's anyway," I offered, looking for any excuse to avoid spending the worst night of my life with Regina.

"Just call. You won't know if you don't call. In the meantime, I'll get you set up in a hotel for the night."

I didn't have time or strength to argue with her so I agreed to the hotel. I left my car right there in her driveway and let Karen take over. She called Randy inside the house with my cell phone and gave him the two-dollar version of what was going on. He offered to take over, like any decent man would, but this was less difficult with another woman. So Karen and I dashed from my car to her minivan and made our way to the nearest hotel. The wind-whipped rain combined with the tears to make me look just like the other storm victims instead of Derrick's victim. We drove out of Queen's Harbor to an almost empty street. Karen sat right up on the steering wheel as if being close to it would help her control the swaying motion of the van being controlled by the early stages of Lily. With the storm bearing down, I didn't have time to pinch pennies like I normally do when searching for accommodations. Two miles from her neighborhood was a Doubletree, so I nodded to Karen that it would be just fine, as she swerved into the parking lot. I had meant to turn the cell phone off after Karen called Randy, but I didn't, and it was ringing again. Derrick's number flashed on the tiny screen. This time Karen pushed the power button. Her index finger pressed against the phone so hard it trembled. She killed the contact temporarily with a force that made it feel almost permanent, and in my heart, I knew she felt my pain.

6

When Karen and I walked into the hotel lobby, it was like a war zone. There were plenty of folks seeking refuge from the storm, so the line was longer than you might expect on a Thursday afternoon in August. Karen fumbled with stuff in her purse while I tried not to break down crying. The tears were welling up despite my attempts, so I just shifted my weight from foot to foot and tried not to make eye contact with anyone in particular.

The receptionist reluctantly motioned for us to step forward since the man in front of us was having problems getting his credit card to accept the charges. It's called maxed out, I thought, as I stepped in behind Karen, not able to deal with the arrogant minimum-wage hotel help.

"One room, queen-size bed, non-smoking," Karen cheerfully announced to the receptionist who obviously wanted to be anyplace but behind the long breast-high desk. She glanced behind Karen at me, rolled her eyes, and nodded her head disapprovingly. I looked down again at Karen's attire and short blonde locks tossed back and laying slicked down to her head from the heavy rain. I giggled at the thought of what we looked like. Cute little blonde chick paying for a room as her ashamed black lover hides in the background. Karen reached for her receipt, signed it, and thanked the lady who should've been slapped instead. Despite my weakened emotional state, I hated the accusations that flew from the receptionist's eyes. I slid my arm around Karen's waist, winked at the assuming receptionist, and mouthed a thank-you sealed with a kiss. Karen was clueless but did ask why the girl suddenly dropped her mouth open and said, "Naw she didn't."

Karen walked me to the room to get settled for a night without sleep. Who sleeps after finding her husband of nearly ten years screwing some woman like she's the last piece on earth? I threw my purse on the bed and flopped down. Karen did the same. As much as she needed to get out of the storm and back home, she really couldn't leave me by myself.

"Go ahead and say it. I told you so."

"I would never say that, Jess. You know I would never say something like that."

"But you did. You tried to tell me. Everyone did. I just kept making excuses for him. I really wanted to believe he was a decent, hard-working man, but deep inside I knew. I knew all along, just didn't know what to do, and I still don't, even with it staring me in the face."

Karen called Randy to check on the kids and let him know she'd be home soon. I watched her cleverly wording her phrases to not give away the fact that Randy was saying things about my situation. This was only the beginning. Everyone would have something to say. And the one I was dreading most was my own mother. When Karen was done with her call, I'd have to check on the boys. While she was wrapping up, I squared my shoulders and tossed my own grief aside to let my mothering instincts take over. Karen hung up the phone and stood to leave. But not before offering words of comfort. As if there was any such thing in a case like this.

"It's not that we didn't like Derrick. We just thought you could do better, and he never treated you like the wonderful person you are."

"I know you tried to get me to confront him about his actions, but after that first time, I just didn't think it would help."

A couple of years after Derrick and I were married, he had started openly flirting with members of the choir at the church where he played the saxophone in the jazz band. He was already working all day and spending too many nights at church conventions for my taste. But when he tapped Sister Freda on her behind right in front of me, that did it. I confronted him about it and he made some lame excuse about encouraging her. She had low self-esteem and asking her to sing a solo was his way of helping her build her esteem. I was confused as to where tapping her behind fit into the esteem building, but he assured me that it was merely a gesture like the ones football players give when they pat each other after a touchdown. I let the matter go and resolved that my own insecurities were playing a role in the matter. The flirting didn't stop, and each year I added another five pounds to my butt and waistline. My self-esteem was suffering, but Derrick never found time to pat my behind.

Karen left after I promised her I would call Regina and check on the boys. I also promised I would sleep, knowing full well I would neither sleep nor call Regina. But I did have to check on the kids. I dialed the number hoping the conversation would go quick and painless. And it did. The line was busy. Before I could hit the power button, the ringing started. Expecting Derrick, I almost tossed the phone without looking at the number. I looked anyway. And I sort of lucked out. This time it was Regina's number.

"Girl, where the hell you at? Derrick calling here acting like a fool."

"I'm at the Doubletree Inn on Atlantic, Karen just left. I caught Derrick with someone," I heard myself say, as Regina started with one question after another, after another.

"Regina, I'll be okay. I just need this time to think, and get myself together."

"I'm on my way," she insisted.

"No please, the storm is getting worse by the minute. You shouldn't be out."

"I'm not staying here anyway. It always floods over here. I was going to Karen's since she's close by. Let me go before they start blocking the roads," she insisted and then all I heard was the dial tone.

I didn't fight it. I really didn't want to be by myself. There was a storm raging outside and my life was falling apart in the confines of a hotel. I needed to figure out what to do next, how to confront Derrick about what I saw, and I'd preferred level-headed Karen, but roughneck Regina would have to do.

Karen, Regina, and I have been friends since high school. We had let Regina into our twosome after she and Karen got into a fight over Randy. When I say fight, I mean fist-slinging, fingernail-clawing catfight. Right there in the hall of San Marco High, Karen and Regina had gone toe to toe. Before I could get help, the two were swinging their arms wildly in that "girl fight" kind of way. Regina's head was swinging from side to side, slinging Jheri curl juice all over the crowd of bystanders that was forming. When Regina finally got her hands on Karen's blonde bangs, I thought it was all over. Karen was outmatched in size, strength, and endurance. The only thing that kept Regina from whipping her behind from one end of Blakely Hall to the other was a backpack. Someone had thrown a backpack down inches from the fight and just as Regina got to smacking Karen real good, she stepped on the pack loaded with at least six or seven textbooks. Her foot came down; she lost her balance and went tumbling over like Goliath being struck by David's sling-shot. With Regina lying on the floor, Karen had time to catch her breath and wipe the blood from her face just as the principal jumped in to break up the crowd. Both girls looked like they had been in fights with alley cats instead of human beings. Besides a few scratches on their faces, the only real injury was the one Regina sustained by tripping over the backpack.

Regina had gone to the hospital to get her ankle treated while Karen and I waited in the principal's office. The school had started this peer mediation–type system and we were the lucky ones to get to break it in. Two days after the fight Regina, Karen, and I were lined up in front of a group of our peers to work out the situation. I sat between the two girls hating every minute of it. In most cases the peer mediation thing was just a joke, but it worked for those two. Turns out Regina wasn't in-terested in Randy at all, she just had a problem with white girls and black guys. Regina already had a boyfriend; she was just being the crusader for the cause of all black women. The peer mediation group made the two girls do a community service project together at the local community shelter and no one really knows what happened except after the project was over, Regina and Karen were close friends. So instead of Karen and me jumping her after school and beating her down, we let her into our group and the twosome became a threesome.

The pounding on the door made me jump. I looked at my watch and what seemed like a matter of seconds was actually enough time for Regina to drive across town. At six feet, weighing in at one hundred sixty pounds, her knock sounded more like a giant slamming his fist against the flabby wood. I opened the door, and as Regina stepped in, my cell phone rang. I threw my hand up to stop Regina from yapping. I answered the phone to the unwelcome voice of my mother.

"Look, Jessi. Derrick is here to get the boys. And I'm not getting in the middle of this. If you all hit a rough spot, you need to talk it out, ya hear?" she insisted, with Derrick asking my whereabouts in the background.

"Mama just trust me. Don't let him take the boys. And don't tell him where I am."

"Jessi, this is childish. Couples have troubles all the time. There's a storm, and these boys need to be home with their parents," she whispered, Derrick still carrying on about none of this making any sense.

"Mama, I'm staying at a hotel. I caught Derrick having sex with someone. I went to his office today to get my checkbook and he was in the break room with a woman. Having sex. Keep the boys and I will call you as soon as the storm is over and I can think straight," I yelled and hung up the phone.

I wasn't sure if she would honor my request or side with Derrick, but I had neither the patience nor strength to deal with it. She'd never supported me in the past, so my mind led me to believe that she would let the boys go and then call me back to tell me all the things I had done to bring this on myself. I could hear the wind pushing hard against the windows. So hard that the curtains moved back and forth. Regina was still standing by the doorway. As soon as I made eye contact with her the tears started again.

"I hate hurricanes," is all I could manage to scream, as Regina flopped down beside me on the bed. And I hoped she knew my outburst had nothing to do with the storm on the outside.

7

If I hadn't known better, I would have thought Regina was the betrayed wife. She jumped back up and was huffing and puffing all over that tiny room. Part of me wanted to do something irrational, like send her to beat him up, but then I thought of how truly ridiculous that would look. I watched her prancing with clenched fist, talking about what she would do to him.

Regina grew up in Jacksonville just like I did, but she spent her early days on the north side. That's how she became so streetwise. The north side of Jacksonville is where you find the housing projects, check cashing agencies, and barbeque ribs that make you wanna slap your mama. Regina's mother died as the result of a domestic violence attack when Regina was thirteen. That's when Regina moved to Orange Park with her aunt and started going to school with Karen and me. Her dad went to jail for killing her mom, and although Regina had gone through endless counseling sessions, she still holds firm to the fact that she's never giving a man that kind of power in her life. After all she'd seen at home, marriage is out of the question.

So now as I watched her nearly coming to blows with the wall, I knew her frustration and anger was about more than Derrick and me.

"You need anything? I got some clothes in the car. You'll

need something to wear tomorrow when you file charges against him," she offers as my eyes fall on the upper regions of her thighs.

Regina has great legs, but I would never be caught in such a revealing skirt. I let the thought pass as I try to think of what kind of clothes she has so aptly brought for me.

"File charges, what kind of charges?"

"Adultery," she belts, and my eyes are pulled away from the hot pink strappy sandals that are actually quite nice, but the heels are a bit too high for getting around in a hurricane.

"Regina, people commit adultery everyday, what kind of charge is that?"

"I know you don't plan to go back to him, not after this. You let that man take advantage of you too long anyway. You are gonna leave him, aren't you?"

"I don't know what I'm gonna do and I don't need you barking orders at me, Regina."

She let it go, although I knew the discussion was far from over. As much as Karen and Randy hated Derrick, Regina hated him more. She said he had those sneaky lying eyes. The kind that only open halfway. My mother always said, "You can see clear through to a person's soul if you look into their eyes." I assumed that's why Derrick never fully opened his; might reveal too much of his dirty soul.

When I had first introduced Derrick to my friends, all Regina could talk about was his Fat Potential. At twenty years old he was tall and in great shape, but Regina insisted he had Fat Potential; the kind of body that with a little age, a lot of sitting around, and home-cooked dinners would turn into gut and booty for days. And in less than two years after we were married, it happened. Derrick's belly lapped over his pin-striped Sunday suits until you couldn't even see the belt. Every Sunday some sister in the church band was loading him up with his favorite dessert or inviting us over for country cooking that only somebody's grandma should know how to do. And if that wasn't enough, there were always those very grateful women he sold cars to. The ones that didn't have the credit to get a car loan, but big enough breasts to get favor from the owner of Happy Motors.

Almost out of nowhere, Regina spun around and pointed the multicolored nail of her index finger right at my face. I jumped back, hoping she wasn't about to poke my eye out or punch me.

"You know she ain't the only one," she whispered, to bring me back to the ugly reality of why I was stuck with her in a hotel room in the middle of a hurricane.

Her comment landed a punch. Not physically, but it hurt the same.

"I'm sure you're right, Regina, but excuse me if I don't exactly feel like running down the list of possible candidates that slept with my husband," I said, as if I were talking to Derrick instead of one of my best friends.

Regina stood and paced again. This time I noticed that she was quite proficient at maneuvering in the high heels.

"You don't have to get ugly with me. I'm on your side. You know I got people, I could make a call. You know I dated that black Italian that time. I say he was just black with good hair, but he said Italian, so I didn't argue. He said he got connections in high places. I could make a call," she added, stopping only long enough to switch her hips to the side and roll her eyes.

"Regina, have you lost your mind? Why are you here anyway?" I said, taking in her whole outfit.

Low-cut mini-skirt, high-rise t-shirt revealing her navel ring, and the pink sandals. I stopped myself from wondering where she was going dressed like that, or worse yet, what she had planned for that get-up.

"I'll go down and get some clothes from the car. It's raining like hell, but it'll probably be coming down worse in the morning. The storm is 'bout to hit land and the eye should be scooting past here by morning," she offered, and I simply nodded.

She grabbed her purse, same hot pink as the sandals, and stomped back out the door. I didn't mean to offend her, but she was working my nerves with her ignorant talk. Regina had a good heart and I knew she meant every word of it when she said she would do bodily harm to Derrick for me; she was just not what I needed. I wanted to ask her to leave, but then it would be just me and that ugly painting hanging over the queen-size bed, and the even uglier picture of what I had seen at the car lot. For now Regina would have to do.

Back when Regina became friends with Karen and me, she was closer to Karen. I just went along with it, since she seemed to need a friend. Over time, I learned more and more about her home situation and our friendship was more like a charity case on my part. I didn't care for her style or way of doing things, but I figured if Karen could stomach it, then I would too. Over time Regina grew on me. Her antics and spicy attire were almost something to look forward to.

Regina had gone to her car and come back into the hotel room with a duffle bag full of clothes and a separate bag with shoes. She had thought of everything. Toiletries and underclothes, everything. It's almost like she had done this kind of thing before. Who knows what to pack when your best friend has just found her husband between another woman's legs? Regina certainly did, I thought as I pulled a Mickey Mouse nightshirt from the bag.

"I'm sorry I acted ugly. This whole thing is just a mess," I said, peeking through the bag to see what else she had.

"Girl, you ain' got to apologize. You been through enough. Get you a shower, and put that shirt on. I'll make a pot of coffee and we'll talk, your style."

"I am glad you're here," I offered, as she went on bumping around the room.

And it was true. Regina has an in-your-face style that can come across harsh if you don't know her heart. I felt bad for being so cross with her when she was only trying to help. I shut the bathroom door and stared into the mirror until I could see past the woman staring back. I blinked away the tears and wondered how long I would have to feel like this. I could still hear Regina moving around outside the door. And the sound of the wind and rain shoving against the window.

I pulled myself from the daze and followed Regina's instructions. The shower helped a little. For some reason I felt dirty. I felt dirty for looking past it all those months. I felt dirty for still allowing him to touch me even though I knew he was messing around. I remember the first time I suspected he was creeping. I confronted him and he tried to cover it by acting like he wanted me so bad. He flirted and toyed with me until I gave in. We made love like a couple teenagers sneaking out against their parents' wishes. He had started trying all kinds of freaky stuff, too. Stuff I suspect he was doing to Minnie and all the other women he managed to drop to the floor in a sexual frenzy. I stayed with him because I thought I was doing the right thing. I wanted to believe it would work itself out. Or maybe I was just too weak to leave. For a woman like me, Derrick was a catch. Handsome, talented, and charm for miles. I've heard his look referred to as "bedroom eyes." Full lips with a thin, almost French-looking mustache gracing the curves of his top lip. And a tiny patch of hair just below his bottom lip. I remember him flicking that patch of hair all over sensitive spots on my body. Thinking about it now made me sick, and I felt the remains of that donut from hours ago. I thought I had thrown all of it up on the street.

I used all the hot water and as the warm liquid turned cold, I turned the water off, toweled dry, and wrapped myself in the warmth and safety of Mickey. Regina was waiting on the bed with hot coffee, just the right amount of cream and sugar. One cream, two sugars. That kind of knowledge only comes from spending time together. She had put on a Daffy Duck nightshirt and motioned for me to sit with her at the top of the bed leaning on the pillows. I wanted to ask what the Disney theme was about, but as soon as she pulled out her comb and a wire brush, I knew we were taking a trip back to a better time. I slid up toward the head of the bed, laid my head on Regina's lap, and she started slowly combing my "badly in need of a style" shoulder-length black hair. I closed my eyes, only wishing we were back in those innocent days of high school.

Days like the many we spent tending Regina's Aunt Emma's garden. Her aunt always insisted on having a garden. She had grown up somewhere in Georgia where they preferred growing their own vegetables instead of just picking up the ones at the grocery store. In any case, the work fell on Regina, Karen, and me. And on this one particular day we were pulling weeds and raking dead stuff out so the fresh plants could continue to grow. Karen and Regina were pulling and I was raking. That is, until the snake curled his long slender body around the garden tool I was holding. Karen yelled first, jumped to her feet and dashed to the house. Regina started yelling to alert me to the fact that the snake was inching up pole·toward my hand. Fear has a strange way of affecting people, and for me it simply meant my brain shut down. I too rushed toward the house, seeking refuge from the slithery reptile. The only problem was that I forgot to drop the rake. Karen was already inside the house, and as Regina crossed the threshold, she looked back and slammed the door in my face. I screamed, wondering why she was being so hateful and leaving me outside to fend for myself. I yelled louder and louder, and couldn't hear what they were saying from inside the house. Before the tears started to roll down my flushed cheeks, Regina snatched the door open, looked me straight in the eyes and said, "Drop the damn snake, Jessi." Within a split second the tool fell from my hand, and I joined them inside where laughter took over the tears.

For whatever reason, that memory brought a smile to my face even with my world falling apart. I deduced that sometimes it's good to have someone to look you in the eye and give it to you plain. It was no mistake that I was spending this very difficult night with Regina.

For what seemed like hours, the storm pounded outside, Regina brushed and combed, and I talked. I talked about it from the beginning. From the day he opened the car dealership and started playing in the jazz band at church. How can you go wrong with a husband who works hard all day and spends his nights at a church? It started with late nights after Bible study, and then the first time he stayed out all night was more than I could make excuses for. I asked him what he could possibly be doing in the name of God, all night long. But I didn't question it since the band was doing so well and the church was standing room only on Sunday mornings with visitors coming from all around. That's the first place I ever saw Minnie. She was one of the many who came from far and near to hear this soulful jazz band with my husband at the lead.

It was a sight to see. Derrick would enter the church sanctuary from a room to the right of the pulpit area. A team of five women and two men would follow him onto the stage and take their places behind the microphones. As a soft melody started at the keyboard just behind the eight-member ensemble, Derrick would blow a low note on the sax to signify his hearing from God. The ladies to his left and right would join in with a higher-pitch moan and then the men followed suit. Within seconds, the lights would flash on the stage area, covering Derrick and the others with bright reds, oranges, and yellows as the drummer, horn section, and guitar players joined the keyboard. Without warning, Derrick and the team would jump right into a soul-stirring praise song that had to make God himself get off the throne and cut a step. I would clap and sing proudly from the front row as jealous sisters peered at me from the left and right. They had to wonder how great it was to be married to a man with such anointing dripping off him like Derrick. Must make for incredible sex. And it did, only not with me.

I had talked to both Karen and Regina about my Derrick suspicions. Of course Karen offered the sensible input that it was about the power. Derrick enjoyed the power, both at work and at the church. It wasn't about the women or sex, but the power. She encouraged me to watch him closely, but instead I got more involved in my work, afraid of what I might find if I really started looking. Regina wanted me to hire someone to watch him. That was out of the question, but one of her suggestions had merit. She wanted me to get a copy of his cell phone bill to see who he was calling regularly. But I talked myself out of it when my own mother told me that I was just an insecure wife trying to find fault in a faultless man. She stressed the fact that Derrick and I had two boys to raise, and my para-

noia wasn't good for them. As much as I wanted to shrug her words off, the last thing I wanted was to hurt my boys. So I backed off talking to anyone else about my suspicions.

As much as I tried to concentrate on being a good mother and wife, the doubts were still there. So I watched our home phone bills for strange numbers, but he had no reason to call anyone with our phone as long as he had that cell phone. I did the paranoid wife thing a few times by smelling his clothes for women's perfume or looking for a smear of lipstick, and checking his pockets. But part of his job was shaking hands and carrying on with people at the dealership, so he always smelled like other people's perfume and cologne. That theory was blown, and nothing interesting ever turned up in his pockets. He covered his tracks very well. It was easy. You don't have to be too smart these days. All you need is a flex work schedule and modern technology and you have all the rope you need to hang yourself in infidelity.

8

"Girl, you could use a manicure, your nails are busted," Regina said, twirling her well-manicured tips in my direction.

Each of her nails had an array of bright colors. Orange and lime green blurred in my eyes as I looked down at my own uneven nubs.

"These nails are the last thing on my mind. So is my hair and everything else about my appearance. Maybe that was the problem. I let myself go . . ."

"Don't you even go blaming yourself for that fool not being able to control his passions. You need to keep yourself looking good for you, not for some man who wouldn't know how good he had it if Jesus himself slapped him in the face."

She was right, but I had long been questioning myself as being the cause for Derrick's distance. When we first met, he couldn't keep his hands off me, but over time, if I didn't have a little bit of self-respect, I would have begged him to touch me. So much had changed, slow small changes you only notice when you wake up one day and find your world crumpled into pieces.

I had put on weight and, for whatever reason, he had taken an interest in exercising. In the last year, his lapping belly was more like a six-pack and I think I had picked up the extra pounds he lost. I even questioned him about spending so much time at the gym when he wasn't at choir rehearsal. He gave the usual religious spill about his body being the temple of God and he should be taking better care of it. As time passed, I started to agree with Mama: it was all in my head. Derrick flirted and liked the power, and the ladies certainly made no secrets about how much they loved him. As lonely nights turned into lonely months, I spent my time with Ben and Jerry's Chunky Monkey and the television remote. Work was my only outlet and as much as my friends tried to get me to take a vacation, I just couldn't see myself rushing off to some wonderful place, alone or with my girlfriends.

"It's almost midnight. He hasn't called back. I know he's either figured it out or Mama told him."

"So he knows. What are you going to do? He's the bad guy, Jessi."

"I'm not going to be able to put it off for long now. I don't think I want to try to work it out. I have no idea how long this has been going on and how many others. He has no conscience; we won't be able to get past this."

"I'm glad to hear you finally talking some sense. I know you think I'm so different from you because I don't want to get married, but this is the main reason. I don't think I could face the hurt of knowing forever doesn't really mean forever, and the same person who tells you how much he loves you could hurt you so bad."

I watched Regina crawl under the covers and doze off. I looked out the window for a few minutes, watching the scene I had witnessed all my life. Blinding rain and wind that bent the palm trees so far I was sure they'd break. Mother Nature's force had started tossing things around, mostly trash and garbage cans that weren't taken inside before the storm. I watched a lid bouncing across the parking lot of the Doubletree. It flipped and pounded the pavement until it slammed into the side of a car. I couldn't make out what kind of car or even the color as the scene blurred and my mind drifted back to my life. I wondered what the first conversation with Derrick would be like. What excuse would he use? What do you say to your wife who saw you having sex with another woman? The tears were rolling again and I could no longer see what Lily was doing outside.

I looked at the clock and assumed it wasn't too late to call Mama. Hurricanes were the one thing that kept her up all night. I called her mainly to check on the boys, but also because I wanted to believe that she was on my side. All along she had not been. But now I needed to know. She answered, not sounding the least bit sleepy.

"Jessi, glad you called. The boys are sleep."

"So you kept them with you?"

"That's what you asked me to do, right?"

"Yes, but I know Derrick can be a handful sometimes."

"Yeah, but he ain't crazy," she giggled.

"Did you tell him?"

"I said enough. He figured it out. He decided it might be best to leave the boys after all," she paused.

I wasn't sure where to go with the conversation. It was teetering on sentimental and that's a place Mama and I never ventured. I was relieved that she still had the boys and Derrick hadn't given her a hard time. The lights flickered in the room. Regina shifted in the bed, turned over, and went back to sleep.

"Looks like the power might go out soon," I said, hoping to end the call with that remark.

"Jessi, what you gonna do?"

"I don't know, Mama."

"Yes, you do. You already plan to leave him. I can tell in your voice."

"Can you blame me? I caught him in the act, Mama. At work, where anyone could have walked in on him. What am I supposed to think?"

"Jessi, sometimes men make mistakes. What if he just messed up? Is it enough to throw away your whole marriage? You got two boys to think about."

"I can't talk about this tonight. I'll call you tomorrow. Kiss the boys for me," I said and hung up.

The conversation hadn't gone the way my heart had hoped it

would. She was not the ally I wanted her to be. But then again she never had been. I was only four when Daddy left, but I remember the change. It's like she blamed me for him not being around. Instead of a loving mother/daughter relationship, it was more like constant measuring with a device that was ever-changing. Over the years the rules had changed so many times. Was I supposed to be a strong woman who looks out for herself, or a good wife who puts her family first? Somehow I hadn't figured it out, and with Lily tearing through the city, that night didn't seem like a good time to dwell on it.

I went back to the window again and stared into the night. There was nothing but blurry darkness. I pulled the curtains shut and crawled into bed beside Regina. She had already created a warm spot, so I cuddled close to her. I felt so alone, so insecure. I needed a friend. It's good to have friends you can be real with, I thought, as I lay awake and counted the stained brown ceiling tiles over the bed.

9

I'm not sure what time I finally went to sleep, but both Regina and I were awakened by the loud noises coming from the room next to us. Those paper-thin walls put us right up close and personal in Melinda and Eric's business. I don't know Eric and Melinda and after hearing them go at it like they were, I was sure I wouldn't be able to hold a straight face if I ever met them. She yelled, "Oh God, Eric" fifty times if she yelled it once. And he wasn't far behind with the "OOO Melinda." And of course they both had to announce when they were coming.

After nearly a minute of "I'm coming" in that high-pitched female sex voice, I wanted to yell, "well come already, dammit." The sounds reminded me of the horrible scene only hours earlier. Derrick and Minnie going at it like two dogs in the street. But before I could get lulled back into those negative thoughts, the wall started to shake. The hurricane was pounding away outside, but Eric was doing the job inside. Regina and I jumped as the picture on the wall came crashing down right beside the bed. The ugly print hit the floor and the flimsy wooden frame broke apart, sending shattered glass in all directions. If I didn't know better, I would have sworn Eric and Melinda's headboard was going to push through the wall and collide with ours. Regina and I giggled and kept listening like two schoolchildren as the couple ended their earth-shattering, head-banging love session. I looked at the broken frame on the floor and then at the clock on the dresser beside the bed. Not yet six o'clock.

"Eric got him a good wake-up piece, didn't he," Regina joked.

We laughed and then got quiet again to make sure they were done. Their room was quiet, it was over. We settled back down on the bed, staring into the dark and quietness of the room. Regina was getting up to clean the broken picture and trying to come up with clever ways to explain what happened to management, when the phone rang.

Karen was calling to warn us about how bad the storm was. I motioned for Regina to turn on the television and sure enough there was a special report on, talking about all the high winds and rain and power out in some parts of the city. I half listened to Karen and watched the flooding and trees down on the television. Regina was making coffee, watching television, and asking what Karen was talking about. I almost wet myself when someone knocked on the door. A loud, hard knock, kind of like Regina banging on the door last night. Obviously a man's hand pounding on the door with more and more force. I told Karen I had to go, while Regina went for the door. I stood in the background trying to hang up the phone, but my hand was shaking. I don't know what I was so afraid of. Derrick didn't know where I was, and if he did, what right did he have to be mad with me?

Regina opened the door expecting to grab somebody and whip his ass.

"Sorry ma'am, just wanted to let you all know that we're on a backup generator right now, but we don't know how long that's gonna last, so we could lose power at any time. Y'all might wanna settle in and ride this one out right here. Ain't safe to travel anyway. If we lose power, we got enough food and stuff in the lobby to take care of everybody for at least forty-eight hours. Thank ya kindly," he chanted and walked off, only to start banging on Eric and Melinda's door.

"We need a vacuum cleaner in here, glass on the floor," she yelled to him as he nodded and continued his wake-up job.

I felt silly for being frightened, but so much crazy stuff that didn't make sense had happened in the last twenty-four hours. Regina closed the door and we both flopped down, watching the weather report and wondering what to do next.

The next logical thing was to call my boss. Any fool could see that coming in to work was impossible, but my reason had nothing to do with the storm outside, but the one inside my life. I phoned my boss at home. He answered lazily, probably still in bed or close to it.

"Hey Jerry, this is Jess."

"Jessi, hell of a storm out there isn't it. Not fit for man nor beast. You should be able to check your stuff from your home computer, that is if the phone lines stay up much longer." He laughed as if he had said something funny.

I laughed too, out of courtesy. You always laugh at the boss's lame-ass jokes. It's in the manual.

"Yeah, it does sound pretty bad out there. I may check on an account or two, but I'm gonna need a few more days off after this storm passes. I've got some business to take care of that requires daylight hours."

"Oh Jess, you know you don't have to ask. Take what you need, and we'll see you in the office in a few days, if our asses don't get swept off to Kansas or something." He laughed again at his equally poor attempt at humor.

I laughed harder, made more pleasantries, and hung up the phone.

"You sure know how to play the man, don'cha. I could learn a thing or two from you. I'd be further in my job right now, if I'd laugh at their stupid jokes," Regina added.

I nodded in acknowledgment of her workplace ethics. It didn't last long; as soon as Skippy came back on, she gave him her undivided. I thought about what I had told Jerry. I had business to take care of. I didn't know what business I was talking about, but the last thing I wanted to do was spend the next couple of days listening to bad hurricane jokes and how storms are a perfect time to get laid. My company sets up networking systems for small businesses and in recent months started helping them make best use of the World Wide Web in promoting their products and services. I'm the only African American and the only woman. I work with five men, so the conversation isn't always stimulating and enlightening. Not that it would be with women either, but I would rather hear the latest on who's sporting falsies than who pulled the upset in Sunday's game.

Regina was still glued to the television as if they were saying something different in each of their storm reports. What else can you say after a while? It's raining real hard, winds are blowing shit to pieces, and it can't last forever. Stay in the house and eat your bread and drink your milk. End of story.

I paced around that twenty-by-fourteen-foot space until I thought I was going to wear a hole in the carpet, rehearsing what I'd say. Regina still sat in front of the set, sipping coffee during the commercial breaks.

"Don't you need to call work or something?"

"You forget I'm a salesperson. I don't have an office. I work wherever I am. Little express hotels usually are my office. I'll check in later today to make sure the building is still intact. Gotta have someplace to go to pick up my check," she declared, putting her attention back on the TV, letting me know the conversation was over.

After another hour of pacing and half listening to Skippy, Regina wanted to go to the lobby to get something to eat. I was just glad to stop pacing around the room, dodging mental pictures of Derrick screwing Minnie right on that concrete floor in the same room we struck a deal with Drew Stanley to expand and include his floundering repair business. It was crazy all the things that came to mind as I tried to put everything into perspective. There was no perspective. He was a nasty dog and that was that, I concluded, still nursing the mental picture of him with Minnie. Between that awful picture and the countless conversations I'd had with both Karen and Regina as to why I should leave him, the ugliness of reality was growing. Regina grabbed the door key card and a few bucks in case they had the audacity to charge for the food, and we made our way to the lobby.

We were shocked by how many people were already down, eating and mingling like we were at some office Christmas party instead of trapped by Mother Nature's fury. I looked around the room surveying who some of the people might be, while Regina aimed straight for the food table. There were a few men who were probably in town on business. They had on dress pants and button-down shirts with their ties hanging freely around their necks like they had been in a brawl. A couple of young ladies standing off in the corner wearing short black skirts with skimpy blouses of sequin and pearl. Call girls who had been left by their paying Johns when the storm got too rough. In Regina's clothes I could have easily fit right in with them. My rather large behind was punishing the seams of a black skirt that I kept tugging in hopes of making it fall somewhere close to my knees. The blouse was cut too low for a woman blessed with a good handful, but I wasn't showing anymore titty than the girls in the corner, so I made my peace to get something to eat and hide behind one of the fake palm trees posing as décor.

Continental breakfast is what they call it in most hotels. An array of danishes, cereals, and fruit. I avoided the pastries, having tasted that chocolate donut one time too many. A few pieces of fruit and a cup of juice were more than enough.

Just as I was about to join Regina, who was gobbling down more than her fair share, I spotted the couple that just had to be Eric and Melinda. The guy looked like a porno-movie reject and his lady had that just-laid look . . . disheveled hair, lipstick all over the area surrounding her lips, and cheeks still flushed from multiple orgasms. I immediately looked away in embarrassment, but the childlike quality in me made me look back. I rushed over to Regina at the buffet table and tapped her on the shoulder.

"That's them. . . ." I giggled and pointed with my elbow.

"Who . . . that's who?"

"Them . . . Eric and Melinda," I whispered, almost ready to burst out laughing.

Regina spun around, drawing attention to us when most of the food flew off her plate, some landing on the floor, a few pieces back on the buffet table.

"Excuse me . . . ,"she mouthed to all the people who were looking at her as if she were some child needing scolding.

"Let's go, fool, before you make another scene."

"Wait, I got to see the man that was putting it on her like that. Might have to get me some," she added, strolling in the direction of the unsuspecting couple.

"Hi, my name is Regina, and this is my friend Jessi . . . I think we're in the room next door to you." She bubbly gestured toward the couple.

I walked up behind her just as Eric nodded his head to acknowledge her, still wondering how she knew our rooms were side by side. He had a puzzled look on his face, but Melinda had turned a bright shade of red, knowing full well how we knew about the rooming arrangement.

"If this storm keeps up, we may be here for a good long time. You two just call us, we'd love a little foursome," Regina winked and nudged Eric. "And sounds like you could handle all three of us . . . ," she added as she pranced off.

Melinda spun around, smacked her lips in disgust, and rolled her eyes. I shrugged my shoulders at Eric, not knowing what else to do. He smiled sneakily, seeing the whole thing as a compliment, and then rushed off to comfort a very pissed-off Melinda.

10

When we got back to the room I chided Regina for getting me into that mess without warning, but she just blew me off and went back to watching Skippy.

"It's pretty bad out there, folks," I heard Skippy say.

No joke, I thought, as I flopped down to take a nap. I had to admit the little game in the lobby had gotten my mind off weightier matters, and as I dozed off I smiled remembering the look on Eric's face when Regina suggested he could handle three women.

My dreams were not as pleasant as the happenings in the hotel lobby. I drifted from scene to scene like a wayward traveler looking for a resting place. From the scene of Derrick and Minnie, to Derrick's hand on Freda's behind, to my wedding day. None of it made sense and I wanted to wake up, but the dreams held me captive. I saw myself walking from the front of the church just after our wedding. I was still in full wedding gear, veil and all. For some reason I went looking for Derrick, and I found him just as I had yesterday. He was thrusting in and out of a faceless person, but he looked up at me and laughed, toying with me, laughing but still humping and grinding this person beneath him. I screamed and tried to run, but there was a door behind me. I couldn't escape. I screamed louder until a hand reached over my shoulder, shaking me and trying to calm me. I looked back and it was Drew Stanley from the car lot, but he was laughing too. The laughter got louder and louder, and Drew was still shaking my shoulder.

"Wake up girl; you must be dreaming, wake up Jess."

I sat up to find Regina shaking me. But it all seemed so real. They were taunting me: Derrick, the mechanic that works for him, they were all in on it. I cried on Regina's lap, trying to let it sink in. It was all just a game; they were all in on it. Regina tried to calm me and assure me that it was a dream, and those people didn't likely know about Derrick and Minnie. It was all just my feelings of being betrayed. I cried more and Regina comforted. But it seemed so real.

After shaking myself out of that funk, I called Mama to check on the boys. Instead of getting into it with me again, she put Joshua on the phone.

"Mom, Jared is trying to get Grandma to let him go outside. We can't go can we, Mom?"

"Josh, you know it's not safe. The storm is passed, but there are a lot of things outside that can be dangerous. Listen to your grandmother. And let me speak to your brother."

"Ma, where are you and why was Daddy so mad when he left last night?"

"Josh, I'm with Aunty Regina, so I'm fine. Your father has a lot on his mind. But don't worry yourself about that; just make sure you stay in that house until Grandma says it's safe to go out."

"Mom, the power went out and Grandma lit candles and told us stories of when you were little. She said you were hardheaded like us," Jared added before I had a chance to say hello.

"I'm sure she has plenty of hardheaded stories about me, but just make sure you all are on your best behavior. I'll pick you up tomorrow. It's not safe to drive yet. Trees and stuff still down on the roads," I said, hoping to justify my absence. Knowing the boys could care less, but needing to fight off my own guilt.

"They'll be just fine. What you want me to tell him when he calls? You know he's gonna call," Mama said, snatching the phone from the boys, and bringing Derrick back to the fore-front of the conversation.

Not once asking how I was doing. Not one question about my well-being. Just what to tell him, as if there was nothing else in the world to consider.

"Tell him whatever you want, Mama. That's what you're gonna do anyway," I yelled, and slammed the phone down.

And as much as I hated myself for it, I knew that the next few hours I would fight with myself on whether or not I should leave Derrick. I would go back and forth from agreeing with my mother, to wanting to break free of the miserable state of conformity. And at the center of it all were the boys. I'd have to make the right decision if for no other reason than their well-being.

11

I couldn't fall asleep later that night when the weather reports were done and the storm was no longer raging. Regina had talked to the folks at the front desk and they were letting us stay on through the night for free. We could all get a good night's sleep and head out first thing in the morning in the light of day. Traveling at night wasn't safe with the threat of downed power lines and trees.

Regina brought food from the lobby. She gobbled hers down and settled into bed. I assured her that I would get some sleep later, but I needed to be alone with my thoughts. As Regina drifted off to sleep, I looked at my cell phone. I started to call him. I don't know why, I just didn't know what else to do. I pressed the power button and nothing happened. The battery was dead. Good, dead battery saved me from myself. And then I reached for the hotel phone.

Regina woke up just in time to see me with the phone in my hand. It was like she knew what I was doing.

"Why do you keep doing this to yourself, Jess? He's no good and you could do ten times better."

"I want to believe that, but sometimes it's hard. I don't have your confidence, Regina. I'm weak and I'm not sure I can do better. And I have two sons to think about."

"You think I'm so strong. I'm not really strong; I just talk loud and throw around a lot of crap so people won't see how afraid I really am. You're the strong one, that's why I cling to you. I'm just talk, Jess, but your stuff is real. You gotta make it through this. Women like me are depending on you. I need to see you survive. You gotta pull through, not just for yourself, but for both of us," she finished and sank back into the bed, clutching the pillow like a close friend, revealing a very personal secret.

The next morning, instead of Eric and Melinda, we were awakened by the shuffling of travelers and businesspeople getting an early start in the aftermath of Hurricane Lily. Regina and I followed suit. We dressed, called Karen, and came up with a plan of action for getting my things from my house and moving me and the boys into Regina's apartment until I could figure out what to do next. I still wasn't ready to deal with Derrick, so we waited until he was likely gone for work before we made our way to what used to me my normal, three-bedroom, single-family home. Now it held nothing more than memories of speculations, insecurities, and long nights waiting for him to come home.

For the life of me, nothing that I was doing made sense to me. I was going into my own house, my friends watching my back in case my unfaithful husband drove up unrepentantly. Grabbing clothes, shoes, and things for the boys, to get us through however long it would take to get the strength to take the next step through this mess.

Karen was driving up in front of the hotel as we walked out the double doors to get into Regina's car, which was parked in a handicapped spot. We got there just in time. A tow truck was backing up to the front fender as Karen sped across the lot and almost ran him over.

"Wait sir, this is my friend's car. She was staying here during the storm. We're going to move it now."

"Sorry ma'am, gotta take it in. Once we get the call, we got to finish the job," he barked back at Karen while still attempting to hitch his contraption to Regina's car. By now Regina had joined Karen and the two were talking at once as the tow man's head went back and forth between the two of them.

"Ladies, I'm sorry. I understand what you're saying, but I can't go back without either a car or the sixty-five dollars your friend would have to pay to get the car back."

"Oh, so that's what this is about, sixty-five damn dollars." Regina leaned in toward the man's reddened face.

Karen stepped in between the two, pulling bills from her wallet.

"Here, this is eighty dollars. That should more than cover you. Come on Jess, we've got to get moving," she said shoving money into the man's hands and walking off.

Regina watched, shaking her head and rolling her eyes as the tow man walked off, glancing back periodically as if watching his back. I begged Regina to let it go, but she followed Karen to her van and got in on the passenger side. She tossed me her keys and asked me to drive her car since she needed to settle something first.

This kind of thing always sent those two into a rage. If I didn't separate them, they'd go back to the two girls slapping at each other like they did years ago in high school. Only this time they'd fight with words. I couldn't get Regina out of Karen's van fast enough. As the tow man drove off, Regina let her have it.

"Is that the way you handle everything? Just throw money at it?"

"Regina, we don't have time for this. Jess needs . . ."

"I know what the hell Jess needs. And I know you need something, too. A reality check. You can't solve everything with cash," Regina yelled as hotel patrons stopped to watch two grown women acting ugly in public.

"I suppose you're about to tell me this is about race and I wouldn't understand because I'm white," Karen yelled back.

"Yeah, I am going to say that. If we were white men, that fool wouldn't have thought twice about driving off without the car and the money, but no, you had to go and pay him—and not just sixty-five, you had to give him extra, like you rewarding him for treating us bad."

By now folks were gathering around asking if everything was okay. Karen and Regina were both getting louder. Karen's face reddened as Regina's lip trembled.

"So that's the solution. Pay them off, just like you did by moving to Queen's Harbor. Live behind the gate and pay enough money and hope they accept your black husband. They'll never accept him or you, Karen."

"Listen, you two fools, my life is falling apart and all you can talk about is a car that almost got towed. Can we get back to the issue at hand before I lose my damn mind?" I barked equally as loud, and stomped off to get into Regina's car.

Karen and Regina stayed in the van to continue their business and three very angry, frustrated, and scared women sped out of the Doubletree parking lot en route to the house I had left two days earlier, hoping to run a few errands before the storm set in.

12

By the time we got to the house, Karen and Regina had finished whatever they yelled about all the way down Atlantic Boulevard. I drove into the driveway first and Karen pulled in behind me. The two ladies got out of the van chatting like they hadn't been at each other's throats just minutes earlier. I watched them as we all walked up the walkway to the front door. I would never understand those two. So different, two extreme ends of the spectrum, but such good friends.

I walked through the front door with Regina at my side. Karen was left at the door to watch for Derrick. I paused several times before actually going into my bedroom, wishing someone would wake me up and this whole mess would not be happening. But it was happening, and Regina was impatiently waiting for me to start packing something. The house felt different this time. When I came back to pick up the two boys earlier, everything was the same. But now, it was as if the place was nothing more than a shell. The furniture was still exactly where it had always been. There were trucks and books spread throughout the den from where the boys had been playing, and a used coffee cup was on the counter. Clearly someone lived here, but there was no feeling, no sense of life. I wasn't sure if it was the house or just my heart that felt void. I walked into my bedroom trying not to look around and see the mental flashbacks of all the days and nights Derrick and I spent there. I tried not to imagine the weeks I spent on bed rest, trying to take care of myself and two twin boys. The place held so many memories, tiny black-and-white images floating around like ghosts ready to haunt me.

"Darn girl, you think you got enough shoes? One woman shouldn't be allowed by law to have more than five pairs of black shoes."

"Yeah, I guess I got a shoe thing going," I responded, glad to hear Regina's words. Words that shook me from the sinking depression.

"And I ain't gonna even start with all them pocketbooks in your guest bedroom. What you do, open a store or something?"

"I might have to sell them to make ends meet by myself."

It was the first time I heard myself say it out loud. Leaving Derrick would not just mean walking away from a dead-end marriage, it meant being alone again. And raising two children alone.

"I'll buy this pair; well, I would if I could get my big toe in them," Regina laughed and went back to the front to check on Karen.

With Regina out of the room and no comical comments about my clothing, I was left alone to my thoughts, my fears. I scanned the room again, but this time no ghostly images, only me shoving bras, panties, and all the stuff from the medicine cabinet into an overnight bag. Enough stuff for three or four days, I thought, as I grabbed the suitcase and threw in blouses and pants, anything to keep me from wearing another one of Regina's get-ups. Today I was decked out in leather. Florida heat is not the place for leather, especially the day after a hurricane.

I noticed Derrick's cell phone lying on the nightstand next to the bed. I grabbed it and hit the guide to check his last ten calls. Two calls to my cell, one call to Karen, two to Regina, two to Mama, and three calls to a number I didn't recognize.

"Her number," I mumbled, as I slammed the phone to the floor.

I picked it back up and dialed the unfamiliar number. She answered. It was Minnie. I knew her voice. The high-pitched squeak with a slightly Southern twang let me know for sure it was her country ass on the other end. I hung up after her third hello. I threw the phone down again. This time with enough force to send pieces flying in all directions.

"Girl, that ain't gonna do no good. You need to do that to him. Slam him to the floor," Regina giggled as she came back in warning me that Karen was getting antsy and we'd better go.

I had wanted to change and put on some of my own clothes, but Karen was right. Derrick could drive up at any minute. The car lot was only five minutes away and he was smart enough to know I'd need to come back for my things and things for the boys. With one suitcase for each of us, an overnight bag, and a purse that would go with all the outfits I'd packed, we drove away from my home, my life, into the uncertainty of life as The Separated. That awkward stage between bad marriage and no marriage.

13

After getting enough clothes and shoes and necessities to last for a few days, Karen, Regina, and I made our way to Regina's place. I kind of felt like a fugitive. I had just stolen clothes from my own house, and now I was off to hide out with my rough-and-tough homegirl. All the makings of a Spike Lee joint, only it was my life, not some silly movie.

As we drove down Atlantic headed toward downtown, I noticed all the debris still scattered along the sides of the road. Yards and parking lots were a mess, just like my life, I thought as I forced my eyes back to the road. There was no trash on the road. Just dark asphalt that led to my new life. Not the life I had chosen for myself, the one that had been forced on me by a simple turn of events. If Derrick hadn't picked up the wrong checkbook, I wouldn't have gone to his job and seen what I saw. I wouldn't be moving myself and my children in with Regina. A sickening feeling came over me as the thought of the little money in my account flew back across my mind and slapped the taste out of my mouth. How would I ever take care of all three of us on my income alone? The thought of Derrick paying child support was one that I didn't want to venture near. I could see his face plastered across the TV screen on one of those public-access stations that broadcast criminals. He'd join the long list of deadbeat dads, and I the longer list of mothers waiting for that monthly check. I felt helpless and I hadn't even come face to face with the adulterer yet.

As we drove along, I deduced that I'd have to make it off my own income. It was not that my income was so bad; it was the fact that I hadn't saved any money since the boys were born. My closet full of Prada and Weitzman represented what should have been a full bank account. But that would all change now. The misery purchases had to go. Those shopping sprees where I would buy two or three pairs of shoes with purses to match, because I didn't know how else to fill the emptiness inside. Derrick had always taken care of most of the bills, which left me to do whatever I wanted with my paycheck. A smarter woman would have hidden a little nest egg for tough times. I vowed to become a smarter woman.

I wasn't excited about the prospect of staying with Regina, but it was my only choice with no money. I wasn't about to impose on Karen and Randy, although they had the space for us. Regina's place made the most sense; besides, she wasn't even in town most of the time. It was the best situation considering the fact that all I really wanted to do was have someone pinch me and wake me up from this nightmare.

And the nightmare got worse. When we drove up to Regina's apartment, Derrick was standing in front of her door looking right at us. We spotted him too late to keep driving. Regina had already pulled into the lot and was about to park when Karen spotted him. She slowed down and hesitantly pulled into the spot marked D-3. Derrick's truck was in the other spot marked D-3, so if running away from my own home wasn't bad enough, I had run right into the man I was hiding from.

Regina offered to handle him, and Karen grabbed her phone to call Randy. I stopped them both, knowing I couldn't put it off any longer. There was no reason to be afraid or upset. I would let him know what I saw and that it was over. I was in control. He was the one who had done wrong, not me.

I got out of the car with my girls each at my side. I stepped over empty milk jugs and a used baby diaper, trying to keep my attention on anything but my unsteady stride.

"Ladies," he nodded, speaking to Karen and Regina.

Neither of them said a word. We all just stood there in front of him.

"I need to speak with Jessi, alone, if you two goons don't mind," he joked, knowing full well we were not in the mood.

"Who the hell you calling a goon, you piece of shit," Regina barked back, stepping closer to Derrick just like he wasn't a man who could easily take her down if he wanted to.

"Regina, I'll handle this. It's okay. I don't mind talking to him. There's really not much to say anyway." I motioned for both Karen and Regina to go inside.

"Just say the word, girl, and I'll put this common Negro right where he belongs, under the bottom of my size tens," Regina growled, giving Derrick the eye as she unlocked her apartment door and went inside.

Karen followed as Derrick and I watched. We both waited until they were inside with the door shut before we spoke. I had planned to speak first; I had rehearsed the speech a hundred times in my head at the hotel.

"Leather, what's up with that," he giggled, checking out my strange attire.

His calmness threw me. He was joking about my clothes and talking to my friends like he hadn't just done wrong. He wasn't acting like a man who had been caught and was sorry. I would end it for sure, right here, right now. But Derrick jumped right in with his speech before I could get my thoughts together.

"Listen Jessi, I didn't come here to deny anything. You saw what you saw. I'm not going to tell you it was the first time or it was a mistake or anything like that, because it wasn't. I'm in love with Minnie and I didn't know how to tell you. We've been together for a while now, and I'm actually glad the hiding and lying is over."

I knew he was still talking. I could hear words, but I felt like his voice was growing fainter with each breath I took.

"I'm not here to ask you to come back. I think we should both go on with our lives. I've already called my lawyer and he's getting the paperwork ready to make the separation legal. I'll have him mail you copies here if you like," he offered, as he walked off, heading toward his truck.

I turned to watch him leave, feeling like I was watching this happen from outside my own body.

"Oh, and by the way. You can do what you want with the house. I'm moving. And I think the boys would be better off with me. So I'll be requesting full custody of them. Boys need their father, you know," he added, and kept babbling something as he hit the alarm to unlock his truck, opened the door, and slid inside.

He started the engine and drove off, not even looking back. My legs wouldn't move. My eyes were glued to the empty parking spot where his truck had been sitting, and now there lay the hurricane-tossed remains of a milk jug and diaper. I had been thinking about child support when Derrick had something more troubling in mind. He wanted to take my children from me altogether. I felt tears, but my eyelids were dry. My chest hurt. The pain felt like a rock or someone's balled-up fist lodged right between my breasts. I wanted to clutch my chest, but my hand wouldn't move. I just stood. I heard the apartment door open. I felt hands on my body. I couldn't snap out of the daze, so I let them guide me into the apartment, to the plush sofa that gave under the pressure of my weight. I sank deep into the fabric of the sofa, and to the lowest place I had ever been in my whole life.

14

I'm sure hours passed as I sat there on that sofa, because both Karen and Regina kept coming over to me with coffee or hot tea. A couple of times they offered food. I couldn't respond. Regina draped a hand-sewn quilt over me and turned the lights down. I assumed she was going to bed. I still just sat. I don't know why my mind wouldn't respond. The gears in my head wouldn't churn. I could see things going on around me, hear sounds, smell fragrances, but I couldn't respond to any of it. I had heard of people having nervous breakdowns before. I always imagined a breakdown being more dramatic, like screaming and crying and fits of rage, but my breakdown was more like a shutdown. My body and soul couldn't handle it, so it all just stopped. And no matter how much stimulation came from the outside, nothing would make it go again.

I don't know when I snapped out of this state, but the next phase wasn't much better. It felt like a state of consciousness half the time and unconsciousness other times. Regina and I would start a conversation and, suddenly, I was someplace else. I tried not to let her know I had zoned, but it was clear I had no idea what she was talking about. I wanted to get past this state, but sitting in Regina's apartment just made it worse.

"Your mama called. Said she let the boys go home with

Derrick. They had school and she wasn't sure what to do," Regina announced during one of the times when I was somewhat coherent.

I nodded at her to let her know that I heard the words, but any further response was too much. And within seconds I was out of it again. The craziness went on for two days and just as I was about to get the strength to make a few decisions, the papers came, just as Derrick said they would. I opened the package, read over the papers, signed them, and re-sealed the package. Regina mailed it when she went out to work the next morning. One week after the storm I had gone from a married woman with a bad feeling in the pit of her stomach to a soon-to-be single woman with no feelings at all.

The thought of the boys with Derrick frustrated me, but I didn't want them to see me in that state. So I told myself they were better off with him. They both loved their father, and in his own way he loved them. He didn't spend a great deal of time with them, but when he did the boys always loved it. I convinced myself that they would be fine with him until I could get myself together mentally. The thing I couldn't put off any longer was work. I had used a couple of vacation days, but with the uncertainty of my future, I decided it would be smarter to save some days for down the road.

I went back to work and tried my best to go on with business as usual. Karen wanted to be by my side more, but Kayla had an ear infection and was keeping her up all night. Regina was being her usual self and I was grateful just to not be entirely alone.

My coworkers were oblivious to my drama, as if they would understand anyway. They were all married and likely doing as much dirt as Derrick if not more. There was no need to mention a thing. I informed Jerry of my change of address and all he could say was, "Sure, lady, I'll make certain the right people get the info, wouldn't want that paycheck held up 'cause of wrong address." Paycheck. No question of why the change of address. Perhaps I'd moved into a huge mansion with all the money I was embezzling from the firm, or leaving my husband of ten years, and couldn't bring myself to move back into the home we had shared together. There was no point in getting into it. To tell them the truth would have just made for one of those long, uncomfortable silent moments where men don't know how to respond. They shake their head and stare at you with squinted eyes of concern, having no clue what to utter. So the smart ones don't say a word. They just shake their head, shrug their shoulders, and pat you on the back and say, "Hang in there, we're here if you need us." Yeah right, I thought, as I sat at my computer trying to clear away the tears long enough to see the screen.

Regina left town again for her usual weeklong field visits. She offered me her place for as long as I needed it. I hated that I needed it. Needy and pitiful were my latest attire. Pitiful because of the way he had dumped me right at my friend's front door. And the thought of him having the boys and going on with life, as if he had done nothing wrong, made me sick. I wondered if he was living with her and the two of them had my boys carrying on like they were some kind of family. Needy and pitiful were turning to anger and rage, at Derrick and my mother.

The audacity of my own mother. To let him take the boys after I had asked her to help me out. She could have gotten their clothes and made sure they got to school. But no, she just gave them up, still taking everyone else's side except her own flesh and blood. I wasn't sure who I'd deal with first, Derrick or my mother, but the sulking had run its course and it was time I did something or I was going to explode.

With Regina out of town, I had time and space to think. To devise a plan to talk to my mother and hopefully find out how to get her on my side. And then I'd have to find out how to get the boys back. They'd have to move into Regina's with me. Not the best situation, but it was all I had for now, with so little money in hand.

Regina's place was small and expensive, but so are all the places downtown. Convenience has a price. Regina's office building is downtown and so are all the good sports bars. Perfect place for a single woman who makes plenty of money and rarely spends more than a few days at a time in any given city. Strangely enough, when she was gone the place felt smaller. Like it was closing in on me. The kitchen and den were one open space separated by the stuff that gave each room its designation. The kitchen was the area with the stove and refrigerator, the area beside it with the table and chairs was the eating area . . . and the den housed a couch, recliner, and TV/entertainment center combo. A few plants, fake ones of course. Not much on the walls. Regina had said paint did the job just fine, why waste money on paintings and junk. So no paintings, no junk, only space and that too was minimal. I tried not to go into her bedroom. There really wasn't reason to. It's not like I planned to borrow any of her things. I made my home on the sofa and on occasion spent all night in the recliner watching Nick at Night until my eyes could no longer focus. And eating. That was a story in itself. I had always turned to the four food groups when things weren't going well. With abundance from each food group, for one more night, I locked myself away from the world outside. Telling myself that strawberries slathered in chocolate still count as a fruit.

15

The next morning, my first order of business was my mother. I couldn't put it off a second longer. I drove straight to her house, not worrying about what I would say, or how it might sound. My life had crumbled in ways worse than I ever would have imagined, and she was no support. I had nothing to lose in confronting her. My hand rapped against her door with the same force that the notion of her taking his side had rapped against my heart.

"I was wondering when you'd show your face," Mama said, as soon as she opened the door.

"Sorry to take so long. I've been in crisis, in case you hadn't heard," I responded without smiling, equally meeting her insensitive tone.

"Come on in. No need to wallow in self-pity. What you gonna do now? Derrick seems to be doing just fine with the boys. And I hear you staying with that wild girlfriend of yours."

"Oh, so you heard something. That's amazing because you never seem to hear me, Mama. I guess you're just not tuned in to my frequency. Is that it?"

"Listen, girl, don't get ugly with me," she said, squinting her eyes and pointing her finger at my face.

"Well, Mama, why don't you help me? I needed you to help me until I figured this out, and you let me down."

"I'm trying to look out for you. You didn't even talk to the man. Just made up your mind that you didn't want to work through this. Bet you let those so-called friends of yours talk you into that," she added, walking into the kitchen.

I followed. Not because I wanted to, but this was the way it worked with us. No pleasantries. Just one long argument teetering on the edge of explosive.

"Not true, Mama. In case you hadn't heard, he doesn't want me. There, I said it. He's with someone else because he loves her and he doesn't want me anymore. So even if I was planning to stick my tail between my legs and go back, he doesn't want me," I screamed, walked back into her living room, and collapsed on her couch.

The last place I wanted to break down like that was my mother's house. I had planned to be strong and lash out at her with painful words or resentment. But all I managed was weak accusations and tears. She stood over me shaking her head as if in embarrassment. The last place I wanted to be was desperate, depressed, and depending on her. But I couldn't move. The only thing I could do was cry. A deep, gut-wrenching cry that hurt my throat. And the last thing I expected to happen while I sobbed on that couch happened, too. Derrick and the boys walked through the front door.

My mother's living room suddenly became about two sizes smaller as Derrick and the boys joined us. I wiped the tears and straightened myself enough to hide my emotions from the boys. Mama tried to hurry them into one of the back rooms before Derrick and I had words, but they weren't hearing anything as they grabbed and tugged at me, talking on top of each other.

Josh wanted to know if I was feeling okay, and Jared asked where I'd been at least three times in two seconds. Derrick was staring at Mama and her eyes were glued to me and the boys. I hugged and assured them that I was okay as hurriedly as I could, but they were not moving along fast enough for Derrick.

"Need to leave them with you for a little while," he said to Mama as if I wasn't sitting two feet from him, with our sons' arms wrapped around me.

"Leave 'em with me. Jessi's right here. Boys, come with me so your mama and daddy can talk," she said, tugging at the boys.

Neither of them let go of me. Derrick poked his lips out and shouted at them with his sternest father voice. I wanted to slap him for being so insensitive. They were uncertain of what was going on, and looking to the only sources they knew for understanding. But the sources were in no position to help them.

"Jared, Joshua, go on with your grandma now. Me and your mama need to settle some things. I'll be back for you in a few days," Derrick added, turning toward the door as if he had someone waiting outside.

Mama walked to the living-room window, pulled back the curtain and smacked her mouth loud at whatever she saw. I assumed it was Minnie or some other woman Derrick had been involved with. She let go of the sheer fabric and looked back disapprovingly at Derrick. He turned his head, but still no shame registered on his face. Even from where I stood, I wondered how he did it. Flaunt his woman right in front of his mother-in-law and impressionable children and still be seen as a respectable man.

The boys clung to me tighter, as if to say, they didn't care what any of us said, they were not leaving this room without knowing their fate. So right there, a week and a half after Hurricane Lily, my family was trapped in my mama's living room with only three tiny bedrooms and a kitchen in one direction and the object of Derrick's indiscretion in the other. No one moved.

"Mama, can we stay with you? Wherever you're staying?" Josh finally said, breaking the uncomfortable silence that had engulfed the room.

"Of course you can," I returned, as the boys gripped me tighter.

I could tell that while all this was grating on Derrick's nerves, it was sending a loud and clear message to my mother. I hoped she was listening. Part of me wanted to walk outside and slap the woman who was still waiting in the car. The other part of me held tight to my boys, realizing there was nothing more important than these next few seconds. The security of their world had been shaken, and they no longer knew where they fit into it all. Just as Lily had tossed and flipped so many material things, my son's lives were tossed as well. And they were hanging on, hoping to find solid ground soon. From Grandma's to wherever they had been with Derrick, and now I had to take them to Regina's tiny apartment. I slid my arms tighter around them and forged a wall of protection, and strength. Although no words were spoken during those few seconds, there was so much said. The glances, the gestures, and the tension letting up to calmness as Derrick spoke up.

"Might be best if they stay with you. But I still need some kind of visitation. Boys need a man around." He paused, as if some invisible string from outside was pulling him.

"I gotta run. Like I said before," he added, shoving through the screen door, "I'm moving on, so you can do whatever you want with the house."

"Bye, Daddy," Josh said, with Jared chiming in to make the words sound like an echo.

"Yeah, yeah, I'll give you fellas a call. We'll get together, okay?" he finished with a smile and continued out the door.

As much as I wanted to protect them from what that really meant, I knew I couldn't. All I could do is love them as much and as hard as I could and trust that the rest would be okay. As much as Derrick liked the idea of having two sons that looked just like him, the responsibility of it was more than he had bargained for. After a couple of days it wasn't cute and fun anymore. It was hard work and it didn't slide out of the way to give him time to devote to his new relationship. So all our lives were tossed and driven during that storm. And now, we'd all have to find some place to plant our feet and start again.

After Derrick's car drove off, the boys let go and moved on to one of the bedrooms to watch television. They had brought the duffle bag in with them. The same one they'd grabbed the day I snatched them from their home during the storm. And as I looked down at the tight-packed bag, I was sure that if I looked inside it would hold much of the same things it held that day. Mama spoke before the first tear dropped.

"You let him throw his woman in your face like that? And have your boys in the middle of it. Jessi when are you going to develop some backbone?" she whispered, looking over her shoulder to make sure the boys had not come back into the room.

"You always find a way to do it, don't you," I added, standing to my feet.

"Girl, don't stand in my house and sass me," she paused, looking back out the door like she was expecting Derrick to return. "Get your friends to help you move your stuff to storage. You and the boys can stay here. I got two extra bedrooms. No need to cram those boys in with you and that Regina girl."

"No, thank you, Mama. I'd rather sleep on Regina's doorstep than spend one night under this roof," I yelled, and called for the boys.

Without hesitation they rushed back to my side so quickly I was sure they had been listening from the back room. They said goodbye to Grandma in unison and we made our way out the door. I left my mama standing at the door shouting about how selfish I was for doing this to my children. As much as I tried to let it go, get into my car, and drive off, she had pushed me too far.

"You sure do have a lot of nerve. Telling me what I'm doing wrong as a parent. You're not exactly a candidate for mother of the year, you know."

"Jessica Andrews, watch yourself," she said, her teeth gritting, her hands balled into fists by her side.

If I didn't know better, I would have sworn she wanted to hit me.

"If my decision ends up hurting my boys and scarring them for life, well, I have to say I learned from the best. You taught me well, Mama," I added, and jumped into the car before I said something worse, or broke down crying.

My head felt like it would explode. My ears felt like a thousand pounds of pressure was pushing against them as I listened to my tires squealing against the pavement in front of my mother's house. As I slammed my foot against the accelerator harder, the car shot down the street like a rocket. The numbers on the speedometer charged upward as I punched the pedal harder. It's like I wanted to do anything to get away from it. But it wouldn't go away. The memories flooded my soul and the faster I drove, the more vivid they became.

The time my mother had taken my teacher's side and insisted that I should take remedial courses instead of the more challenging college preparatory ones. I wasn't smart enough. The high school prom where I had wanted so much to wear that spaghetti-strap dress, but she insisted that my shoulders were too meaty for anything that delicate. I wasn't dainty enough. And when I married Derrick, she acted as if I should be grateful to have him. I wasn't good enough. There were too many times to face. The scenarios slammed against my brain like a thunderbolt. I hadn't realized that I had been holding all of them inside for so many years. And they had piled up. One on top of the other. But even with each new challenge, I had had hope. Hope that she would for once stand up for me. Even if I was wrong. For once, she would take my side. Join my team. But she hadn't. Not once. No support, no apology. Just more indignation.

I pressed my foot against the brake as I approached the stop light. The yellow turned to red, and the car stopped. The memories stopped, and in that second, I lost hope. I lost hope that she would ever stand by me. And in that second, I let it go. I stopped hating her. But most importantly, I stopped needing her approval.

16

Most folks were still talking about Hurricane Lily because of all the damage she caused, but she was etched in my mind for entirely different reasons. Since Derrick left the house part up to me, I talked to a real estate agent and got the ball rolling on getting the property listed. The boys and I were camped up at Regina's and I was dodging phone calls from my mother. Although I knew Regina wanted her bachelorette pad back, she never made us feel unwelcome. I encouraged myself with the fact that in a few weeks I would have enough money saved to get an apartment. But for now, all I could do was move my belongings from my old house into storage.

Regina and Reginald, her latest piece of man candy, had agreed to help. Karen and Randy got a sitter and spent the entire day packing and cleaning. Everyone had a role to play. Regina and Reginald were responsible for the moving truck. They rented a truck, packed everything, and got it unloaded at the storage unit. I watched as mattresses and headboards, along with clothes I had forgotten I had, were carted from the haven I had known for almost ten years. I worked as hard as I could to keep my true emotions inside. Some things held a special place in my heart, and my chest felt tight as we packed those. But for the most part, the stuff was only a painful reminder of the past, and I was glad to toss it into the junk pile marked to go straight to the landfill. With blue jeans, sneakers, and fried chicken, we all worked until our bodies gave way to fatigue.

Nightfall had closed in on our dwindling productivity; the house was an empty shell, clean but void of any signs that life ever took place there. Void of any signs of a couple doing the things happy families do: eating meals, making love, paying bills. Derrick had moved his things the day after he dropped the boys off to me at Mama's. He had also not been seen since that day. I'd give it a few more days, and he'd resurface. I'd let him see the boys and that would put a smile on their faces that would last until the next time he started feeling guilty. It's what we'd do. He had been right in one thing. The boys needed their father. Even if they didn't get much of him. They needed that little.

"If I see one more pair of shoes, I'm going to throw up. Must be five hundred pair, and I know you've never worn those orange ones with the fruit-scented tassel," Randy added, as we closed the rental truck with the last load.

"Girl, I told you. Start your own shoe store, you got the inventory," Regina added, as Reginald and Karen all nodded their heads in agreement.

Yeah, I'll go start a shoe store; what else do I have to do, I thought, as I dragged my fat behind into Karen's truck and turned my head away from the house, not wanting it to end like this.

With darkness taking over the evening sky, everything I owned was locked safely away at the "We Store It" bin number 857. I watched as Randy slid the door down, latched it and put the heavy-duty lock on. He handed me the key to the lock and the paperwork from the "We Store It" people. A list of rules and regulations for getting your stuff back. I folded the paper twice, wrapped the keys inside, and folded again. No point in separating the rules from the keys, I thought as I shoved it into my purse and got into the truck with everyone else.

We all went to Karen and Randy's for dinner and relaxing. Karen ordered goodies from the clubhouse while Randy fired up the Jacuzzi and sauna. The temperatures were too cool in early September for a night swim, but none of us had the strength or energy to do much more than eat and chill.

When the food arrived, Karen and Regina set everything out on the lanai while Randy and Reginald grabbed drinks and went into the sauna. That left the Jacuzzi for the girls. I watched my best friends in the world working, laughing, and relaxing in the midst of one of the most challenging times of my life. With so much going bad, this was good. Country-club food, lying back in the lap of luxury, and losing myself in the comfort of love that had stood the test of time. We giggled and gobbled in shifts. Karen left Regina and me wolfing down food while she took a shower. When she returned, Regina could not resist comments about her skimpy two-piece.

"Lord, I know you don't call that a behind."

"Regina, you're just jealous."

"I might be jealous of a lot of things, this awesome house, that Lexus truck you drive, and your fine husband, but I got you in the booty department. It's a shame you ain't givin' that black man no more than that to hold on to."

With that comment we all fell over laughing.

Regina grabbed her swimwear and left to take her shower and show us some real behind. As Karen and I sat around the Jacuzzi eating Thai shrimp and sipping margaritas, it seemed like the perfect opportunity to ask her about her relationship with Regina.

"It's strange, really, but Regina is like an equalizer for me. I admit seeing things one-sided; I see them from the only side I know. But I don't want to be blinded to things that hurt Randy because those same things will one day hurt my kids. Regina helps me keep it real. She's extreme and over the top, but I need that. We give each other perspective neither of us would have otherwise."

"But you fight like dogs sometimes and then you turn right around and act like you can't get enough of each other. What's that about?"

She paused, crinkling her forehead before speaking.

"Love, I guess. I guess it's about love. We made a pact years ago to always be real with each other. Even if we couldn't be real with anyone else in the world, we'd be real with each other. That's how we roll," she said, mocking Regina.

I laughed at her attempt at slang, but more at a side of her and a side of Regina I had no idea existed.

"You think she's serious about Reginald? He seems like a nice guy," I asked draining the last drop from my glass.

"Who can tell with Regina? Has she ever been serious about anyone?"

"Guess you're right. But he's kind of cute and definitely sweet on her. Somebody had better warn the boy. Regina doesn't do long-term," I added, and stood to leave.

Regina walked back in to catch the end of our conversation. She didn't bother to defend herself or offer explanations. With more drama and alcohol than I needed for one day, I made my way upstairs for a shower while the two most unlikely friends in the world pointed at their reflections in the lanai mirror, arguing about whose behind would best satisfy a black man.

17

Although I'm usually a detail-oriented person, I left the details to Karen and Regina and focused on the fact that getting away might be the best thing for me. The girls had been begging me to take a trip for more than a year now, but with everything that had happened, it seemed like a perfect time wouldn't be on the horizon anytime soon. I agreed to go, hoping that a change of scenery would do the trick. Although it wasn't cold in Florida, I figured I could use some warmer temperatures and sandy beaches to help lift my spirits out of the dismal swamp of separation. With that, Karen and Regina made vacation plans, and I tried to make myself want to go.

I had finally told the guys at work that I was separated and I got just the response I knew I would. That blank stare and head shake. I regretted telling them the moment the words came out of my mouth, but my regret heightened each time those fools mentioned fixing me up with their one and only politically correct black friend. I shut them all up one day when I announced that I was already dating and he was a white guy. That got an even more dumbfounded look than when I announced my separation.

The night before our flight on the vacation of a lifetime, Regina, Reginald, and I ventured to the North Side for some of

Jerome's pork ribs smothered in barbecue sauce and grease. Regina was right at home when we drove up to the eating establishment that looked more like a storage shed. Reginald hit the alarm on his BMW twice, showing his obvious fear of being out of his element.

Reginald had been transferred to the Naval Air Station in Jacksonville from Rota, Spain. He had been away from areas like the North Side for too long and the whole idea of leaving the comfort of San Marcos and the downtown area made him too shaky.

"If you hit that alarm one more time, the thieves will surely strip it just to show you how meaningless that little contraption really is. Where there's a will, there's a way," Regina teased.

"Yeah, and I have a will too," he added, laughing and double-checking the doors in case the electronic device failed.

Jerome's ribs are known throughout Jacksonville and surrounding areas, but most people who don't live in the area get them during daylight hours.

"Gonna eat it here or take it wicha?" the sweaty woman splattered in grease and barbecue sauce behind the counter asked politely.

"Oh, might as well eat it here, so it'll be good and hot. No need to drive all the way back cross town," Regina answered, without consulting Reginald or me.

Somehow the counter lady knew she was joking. She chuckled a little, grabbed "to go" plates and continued talking to Regina as if she were the only person in the place.

"Want the special? Got ribs, greens, and corn on the cob. Corn bread comes with it and tea 'less you want a Pepsi."

"Sounds good. Tea will be fine"—Regina smiled—"we'll take four."

The counter lady smiled, showing her lack of front teeth but no lack of hospitality as she plopped piles of food onto the Styrofoam plates until the lid would barely shut. I looked over at Reginald, who was still peering at the door as if listening for the sound of his car alarm.

I wanted to laugh at Reginald, but I wasn't much more comfortable than he. His tough military exterior was gone. His soft, handsome features gleamed through the panic and fear on his face. Formerly a navy man, Regina had a picture of him when he wore the close haircut and bare face. Now he was sporting dreads that fell just below his shoulders and a well-trimmed mustache and beard. His deep-set brown eyes darted to and fro as the counter lady and Regina kept talking. In his Tommy shirt, Levi's jeans and Timberland shoes, he was downright good-looking. He glanced at the door again and flipped one of the dreads out of his face. Regina ought to be ashamed of herself for leading him on. Reginald caught me staring, so I covered by acting like I was paying attention to Regina and the food purchase.

"Four plates, who's the fourth one for?" I asked since there were only three of us.

"Randy, of course. Boy ain't likely to get no good soul food at the country club," she laughed, and handed the perspiring lady two twenties and a wink.

The lady smiled, put one twenty into the register and the other into her half-ripped pocket on what used to be a white apron. Reginald was already opening the door by the time Regina and I grabbed the plates. The alarm beeped twice and we got back into the car just as a black Humvee pulled up. Reginald's lip dropped open as he waited to see who would get out. The truck sat there for a couple of minutes before a huge man got out and lumbered into the rib shack. I had no idea who he was, but the smile on Reginald's face meant it was probably some football player. We cruised by the Hummer slowly, taking in the full view of the vehicle. The truck was almost bigger than the restaurant. And the driver was, of course, larger than life.

We dropped off saucy soul food at the front gate of Queen's Harbor, Karen and Randy's neighborhood. The gate attendant looked at the stained paper bag, but never inquired about its contents.

"We'll see that Mr. St. Clair gets this. Thank you and have a nice evening," he smiled, as we drove off laughing at the thoughts that were likely going through his mind as he stared at the bag, too afraid to inspect the contents.

Reginald dropped me off at Regina's place. I was staying there because it was closer to Karen's than Mama's house and everything was closer to the airport than Mama's house. The two of them proceeded to his place for the evening. It was no secret that Reginald had it bad for Regina. We all told her that the first time we went out as a group. The way he looked at her said it all. My mama used to say a man's "nose is open," when he looks at a woman like that. Derrick had sworn Reginald was just "pussy whipped," since Regina was too hard for a man to fall in love with. I disagreed. That boy's nose is open and Regina had better be careful before his kindness and affection start to chisel her rough edges.

Regina proudly let it be known she was going to his place to get some "goodbye lovin." She didn't want to keep me awake with all the noise, so she was going to stay at his place for the night. That was perfect for me. A tummy full of good cooking and a quiet apartment just hours before the vacation I needed and almost wanted.

Daybreak didn't come a moment too soon. I'm not sure whether it was the soul food or Derrick demons, but I tossed and turned all night. One crazy, meaningless dream after another. Most of them ended with me running from or to something. I could hear the busy sounds of commuters making their way to the office buildings that landscaped the downtown area. Engines revving and horns honking as the city came alive yet another day. I looked at the clock on the microwave in the kitchen and, as I suspected, it was past time for Regina to be back. She was supposed to get back by 6:00 to pick me up and drive to Karen's. Randy was going to drop us off at the airport. But at nearly 7:00, no Regina. I lifted myself from the couch and stretched enough to get the kinks out of my back. Couches aren't made to sleep on. A nap maybe, or perhaps a few hours while the TV watches you late at night, but not all night.

I grabbed the phone to get in a quick call to the boys. They were wide awake with the television blaring in the background. Mama ran down the list of everything they had eaten for breakfast. I teased her about spoiling them and gave my goodbyes and kissing sounds through the phone to each of them.

I had hoped to get through the conversation without an argument, but that would not be the case.

"Mama, I know you think a vacation is an irresponsible thing to do right now, but I disagree," I said, shoving last-minute things into my bag.

"You just let those silly girls talk you into anything, don't you? How could you rush off someplace and not even know where you're going?"

"Listen, Mama, the trip is booked, our flight leaves soon. I have to go. I'll call you when I get there," I said and hung up.

I could just see her staring at the phone, surprised that I had actually hung up on her. I couldn't help but laugh and wonder what was running through her mind. Whatever it was, I couldn't let it matter anymore. I tossed my thought in another direction as I sat on the couch for another few minutes thinking about the strange turn of events. With ten years of marriage under my belt and two wonderful twin boys, at thirty three years of age, I was basically nowhere in life. No money and living in a friend's cramped apartment. How does it happen, and does anyone ever prepare for such events? I hadn't, but as days turned to weeks, the dust was settling and we were all getting into our own little routine.

Regina was out of town most of the time, which meant the boys and I had full run of the place. And Mama's main beef was about me going back to church. Since Hurricane Lily, I hadn't stepped foot inside my church or anyone else's, and to Mama that was just unheard of. No matter how big a sinner you are, one day out of the week isn't going to kill you, she would say. She had only pressed me about it once, and my excuse was the fact that Derrick was still there, playing his saxophone and sitting in the congregation beside his new woman. There was no way under heaven I would venture back into that camp and face the accusations and strange looks. As much as Mama rattled on and on about it being good for the boys, I held my ground. I agreed to look for another church, but there was no way I would walk back into a place that let a man treat his wife the way Derrick had and go on as if nothing had happened.

With vacation only hours away, the last thing I wanted to do was get down in the dumps again about the things that were not going right. So I got off the couch and gathered my things beside the door, on the slight chance that Regina would not be late and we would still catch our flight.

By the time I finished my shower, dressed, and had my morning Coke, Regina was sprinting through the door.

"Girl, that Reginald is something else."

"Spare me the details. Karen will be calling any minute wondering where we are. What time does the plane leave?"

"I think ten o'clock, but we should be fine. It's vacation, anyway. You can't be late on vacation. There is no schedule," she added, throwing suitcases toward the front door.

"Tell that to the pilot flying the plane that's supposed to take us to . . . by the way, when do I get to find out where we're going?"

"When we get there," she laughed, running out the door with bags thrown over her shoulders like dead bodies.

The morning commuters were off the roads by the time we left for Karen's. Sure enough, my cell phone rang. A frantic Karen wanted to know what could have possibly held us up.

"Brothers, girl, you know how they are in the morning," Regina yelled loud enough for Karen to hear her.

Karen laughed, but my money says she had no idea what Regina was talking about. Randy was black but far from being a brother, I thought, as we raced across the bridge headed toward the suburbs.

18

We were running late thanks to Regina. She and Randy tossed bags from Regina's car into Randy's truck, and before Karen and I could exchange pleasantries they were motioning for us to get in. Regina got into the front seat, Randy and I slid in back with Karen. After moving a couple of toys and sweeping off cracker crumbs, I begged Karen to tell me where we were going. She refused, and all I could hope is that they packed the proper shoes for the trip. There's nothing like going someplace and your footwear doesn't do the job. I smiled, as I thought of the possibility of not needing shoes on some tropical island in the middle of nowhere. A smile stretched across my face as I thought about the tasteful bathing suit I had slipped into my bag, a black one-piece that flared out at the bottom to hide the wide hips and bulging cellulite. There is no way I would leave a bathing-suit decision to Regina, whose motto on the beach is "less is more."

"Who's with the kids?" I asked Karen, since I wasn't getting any trip details.

"Usual sitter. Ms. Monahan. She cleans and cooks, too. Wouldn't want to leave my children's nourishment in the hands of my wonderful husband," she teased.

"I heard that, lady," he returned, glancing into the rearview and shooting her a quick kiss.

The gesture made me both sick and hopeful, so I pulled my attention from the lovebirds to my exciting vacation, or pending doom. Who knows what to expect with Regina and Karen in control? As we pulled up to gate five at the airport, I was almost excited. As excited as you can get when you're homeless, your money is nonexistent, and your former husband is in love and moving on with a woman half your size.

No sooner had Randy stopped the truck, than they were calling for our flight to start boarding. The mad dash started. Randy and Regina looked like the old O.J. commercials as they flew through gates and passed long lines of businessmen and nasty-nosed kids. Karen and I brought up the rear with bags in hand. By the time we got to the boarding area the receptionist was waving for us to hurry, like we hadn't already run ourselves to death to get there.

I'm not even sure I remember takeoff. I was still trying to catch my breath. When we were finally in the air I shifted and twisted, trying to get comfortable. We were riding coach, so space was not plentiful. The flight attendant started with her spiel and I had all but tuned her out until she mentioned Chicago. It kind of made sense. We would catch a changeover flight out to Chicago to someplace tropical. I relaxed and enjoyed the journey.

When we reached Chicago, just as I thought, we rushed to another gate for our changeover flight, headed to Alaska. When I realized the destination, I stopped dead in my tracks and just stood there. Passengers were boarding and Karen and Regina were tugging at my arm. I waited until the last second for them to laugh and tell me they were pulling my leg. But there was no laughter. Only one flight attendant with a bad attitude as we boarded the plane headed to Alaska.

Regina and Karen ignored me for the duration of the trip, but they couldn't avoid it forever. I wanted to know what the hell kind of vacation they thought we were gonna have in Alaska, but then again I had left everything up to them. Neither of them would make eye contact with me. They sat back tossing peanuts and swigging Bloody Marys. I let it slide since I had enough pride not to make a scene on the plane. I still held out hope that the stewardess was in on the joke and they were only tricking me into thinking we were going to Alaska.

Sure enough, when we landed we were in Alaska. It wasn't some joke they had paid the stewardess to play on me. Those fools had actually planned a trip to Alaska. We got off the plane, ran to baggage claim, and then met some old man with a sign that Regina seemed to recognize. He waved us over and loaded the trunk of a car that was as cold inside as it was out. I watched the thick clouds that formed as words came out of their mouths. He mentioned that the ride was an hour long and I wondered when the old fool planned to turn on the heat.

"Okay ladies, this isn't funny. Please tell me there is some kind of mistake," I insisted.

Karen looked concerned, but then shrugged her shoulders at Regina and went back to looking around at the sights as we bumped along in the car. I made sarcastic comments periodically, but Regina and Karen kept ignoring me. So we rode in that cold boxcar, and after ten minutes I assumed the heater had likely gone someplace else to get warm. I was so shocked by the strange turn that my dream vacation had taken that I didn't notice much about the area except it looked like any other United States city. Office buildings and department-store chains and restaurants just like any other place. As we made our way from the airport, through the city, out of the city, and away from civilization, I was sure Regina had nothing to do with picking this destination. Regina liked adventure, but her ideas always centered around good-looking men and marathon shopping sprees. None of which we'd find in Alaska. I was sure of it. I looked back up front at the driver. No, Regina did not do this, I decided. This was definitely the brainchild of Karen St. Clair, I thought, as I glared in her direction, wondering how my friend of so many years could possibly think Alaska would make me happy after the hell I'd been through.

19

The drive from Anchorage to Palmer was scenic, but I spent most of my time listening to the driver talk to Regina and Karen about the hunting and fishing in these parts. I made up my mind that these two women did not drag me all the way to the middle of nowhere to hunt or fish. There had to be some luxurious resort with the amenities of Club Med. But the more we drove, I had to face the reality that luxury was not lurking around the bend in Palmer, Alaska.

"What part of the property are you gals staying on?" the driver questioned. I listened, trying to learn anything I could about this trip that was not shaping up like anything I imagined in a vacation.

"We're at the Wolverine Chalet, it says here," Regina mumbled, looking over what must have been the paperwork they used to book this awful trip.

"Oh yeah, nice place. You'll like that one. Kind of cozy, mostly couples use it, but you three gals oughta enjoy it, too. Nothin' like getting close to nature to get your gears churnin'," he added, as he stopped the car in front of a two-story, three-bedroom chalet.

I learned that much as Regina read more of the paperwork.

"That one there's yours. Should be full of gas," the driver

motioned toward an old beat-up gray sedan sitting in front of the chalet.

I could clearly see that the tires had more mud than tread on them. The paint was chipped on parts of the passenger door and the hood didn't look like it would shut all the way.

"So we have our own car," I added sarcastically, letting the girls in on my apprehension about our arrangements.

They ignored me. Driver included. He unloaded suitcases from the trunk and handed over the keys. Regina seemed to be taking the lead, which shocked me since this looked more like a Karen kind of vacation. As we walked toward the chalet, I remembered seeing places like this while surfing the net for vacation spots in the past. I've always been curious about spots in the woods with little to no modern conveniences. I've also wondered about the people that pay money to stay at places like this. And now, I had become one of those people, I thought as I navigated the four steps that led onto the front porch of the structure that looked like a triangle sitting on top of a square with legs.

When we first walked into the chalet, my main goal was to seek out standard living necessities. We entered the first level through a door that led directly into a large sitting area with fireplace. To the right was the kitchen, also large and open. Big wooden table separating the kitchen from the sitting area. The table could easily seat ten to twelve people, and it seemed more in the way than an inviting eating spot. To the left of the door was the stairs that led to what I hoped were three bedrooms and not three doorways back out into the wild. I didn't bother to rush up and check out the bedrooms, because if they were crappy, the large plaid upholstered sofa in the sitting area would do just fine. I had gotten used to couch sleeping. There was a bathroom just off the kitchen with normal bathroom stuff: sink, toilet, and shower.

"Wood's on the porch," the driver announced as he made his way back out the door. Wood on the porch could only mean one thing: Those weren't gas logs in that fireplace. Regina and Karen said goodbyes to the driver as I gave the real wood a closer inspection. Regina continued reading off the other amenities from the brochure.

"We not only have our own vehicle, but our own boat, and canoe, there's an outdoor tub, picnic tables, barbeque grill, and horseshoe toss."

I was waiting to hear something that remotely interested me on that list, since this was supposed to be a vacation centered around my pain and trauma. The papers flew from Regina's hand onto the coffee table next to the huge couch, signaling her joyful list of amenities was done. With that I made my way upstairs, hoping to find a decent place to lay my head, adequate lighting for reading, and a bathroom that was at least as nice as the one downstairs. The stairs creaked under my weight; faded oak slabs that led to the triangle part of the chalet.

Regina yelled up the stairs for me to take the first room at the top of the stairs. It was supposed to be the nice one, the one with everything. I hoped everything didn't include too much of the wildlife we were going to be hunting and fishing for. I mumbled an unappreciative "okay" back down, and pushed the door open to the Good Room.

To my surprise, it was better than good. The king-size bed was clearly the attraction of the room. There were fluffy pillows lining the headboard of the bed, a beautiful hand-sewn quilt at the foot, and extra linen, towels, and bedding lying on a trunk at the foot of the bed. I walked through the room to a huge bay window with a bench in front and the most breathtaking view of Wolverine Lake and majestic mountains. I flopped down on the bench and got lost climbing one of the mountains. Something about the scene brought a tear to my eye. It looked more like a painting than the view out of a bedroom window. The huge mountain on the other side of the lake cast a shadow that gave the lake a ghostly hue. There was a fog hovering over the lake as the temperatures outside dropped in anticipation of nightfall.

I guess I had been gone too long for the girls since they stormed my room, both of them almost out of breath.

"I'm not gonna jump. I promise," I joked, as I motioned for

them to join me on the bench to see the view, the picture that only God can paint on the canvas of a bay window in Palmer, Alaska.

We sat on the bench until the sun faded behind the huge mountain. There was no curtain at the window and there shouldn't have been. There is no way anyone would ever want to block out that scene. Karen had gotten up to use the bathroom, while Regina and I talked about what to do for dinner.

"You have a sauna in your bathroom," she yelled. "I'm serious, get in here, there's a real live sauna in this bathroom."

We all then sat in the bathroom for the next thirty minutes trying to figure out how to use the sauna, and discussing all the times we'd need to use it. I was sure to need it if I did anything close to hunt or fish. Then Regina decided to let me in on the most adventurous part of the trip. In three days, we would be kicked out of the wonderful chalet with the lovely view and sauna . . . and made to live in a camper. Part two of our paradise vacation is a tour of the area in a camper. It's called the combination package, and Regina thought it sounded interesting when she was booking the trip with the travel agent.

So I had less than seventy-two hours to enjoy this setting that I had decided I could live with, to tackle life in a Class A motor home enjoying a tour of the Denali National Park and taking a glacier cruise. Somehow the glacier cruise concerned me. I thought the idea is to keep boats away from glaciers, but I was committed to trusting my friends with this one, and I would do everything I could to enjoy it.

Karen's and Regina's rooms were adequate. Regina's had a queen-size bed with patchwork-style comforter, dresser, and small chest we were all afraid to open. Karen got the kids' room that always comes with a set-up like this; two twin beds and an even smaller dresser. There was a view from both their windows, but it was just the front of the chalet, an overhead shot of the car that came along with the paradise vacation. We unpacked and went to find out if in fact that car was there for anything more than decoration. Turns out there was more tread under that mud than I thought. The hood was closed, just buckled a little in the middle to make it look ajar from the side. The paint was chipping and underneath was an aqua color. Upon noticing that, I was glad for the dull gray. With only a few tries, the engine turned over and we all sat there like icicles frozen to the edge of the roof on a house. Karen was in the driver's seat and informed us that the car needed to warm up first and if we drove it cold, it might not be so nice and start for us next time. I sat quietly trying to imagine anything warming up in Alaska, even in early September.

20

We hit the first little diner we found in Palmer, assuming there might not be too many spots for getting a hot meal. The locals were just like locals in most small towns. They all stared at us as we walked through the door, took our seats, and ordered our food. It's like they thought we were going to burst into flames or something. They didn't even look away when we made awkward eye contact with them. And just when my pulse was about to start racing, an older man in camouflage sitting across from a slightly younger lady threw his hand in the air and smiled broader than if he'd just won the lottery. All three of us started waving and grinning at that couple and then at the five or six other patrons in the diner.

"Evening, ladies. Where you from?" the waitress bellowed, causing all our arms to drop back to our side and grins to subside.

"Jacksonville, Florida. We're staying at the Wolverine," Regina announced, as the lady started nodding and placing menus in front of us.

"Nice place. The Winslows own that one. Good people. You taking the camper out or just playing it safe in the chalet?"

"Oh yeah, got to hit the road," Regina chimed in, smiling and nodding as hard as the waitress.

"Florida," she yelled across the room loud enough for all the others to hear.

They all nodded and smiled again. I heard a few say "welcome," and I smiled back, feeling more like I was visiting old friends than vacationing in a foreign land.

"Emily's my name. Live just up the lake from the chalet if you need anything," she chanted and walked off to get our food.

By the time the food arrived, everyone in the place had come over to say hello and tell us about themselves and life in Palmer. The food was hot and the portions generous. We ate and started the goodbyes as we paid the check.

"Is there a store nearby, some place we can get the basics?" Karen asked as Emily shook her head from side to side and motioned for Daniel, the cook, to get some things from the back room.

He came back with bread, milk, cheese, eggs, and bacon. Regina unashamedly asked for coffee and sugar, so Daniel threw in both. He then pulled out a few dusty cans of vegetables to complete the grocery-shopping list.

With food to feed three wilderness women and coffee for our black Grizzly Adams, we got back into our car and headed toward paradise. Not exactly my idea of the perfect vacation, but it wasn't all bad. I had imagined hot sandy beaches, with cool ocean waves rippling up to the shore and tanned, equally hot men serving us tropical drinks with umbrellas. But glaciers and moose in Palmer, Alaska, would have to do for now.

As soon as we got back to the chalet, I put in a call to Mama. I was shocked that she too had been kept in the dark about the vacation spot.

"Alaska. Those friends of yours are crazier than I thought. What you gonna do in Alaska? You don't even like cold weather!"

"It's not all bad. The place we're staying is nice. I'm not too sure about the activities they have planned, but we'll see."

"Derrick's coming for the boys tomorrow. Unless you say otherwise," she said, emphasizing the word "you."

"That's okay. Anything special planned?"

"He said he has tickets for the Jaguars game."

"That'll be nice. Boys will love that," I said, only wishing that Derrick would choke and die instead of land tickets to a professional football game for himself and his sons.

But the calmer, rational part of me forced the mean, angry part to only verbalize positive things.

"Make sure they have something to put on their heads. And plenty of clean underwear. Derrick doesn't always check."

"I've done this before, you don't have to tell me how to take care of my grandbabies. Alaska, I hope you're satisfied. I told you something is wrong with those girls," she added, and then hung up without saying goodbye.

The first lesson I had learned after being in Alaska for only a couple of hours was that I missed my family. The boys, not Mama, and certainly not their lowdown dirty daddy. With that thought, I agreed that it was good to be away. Even if it was Alaska.

21

As soon as my head hit the pillow, I was lulled off into dreamland. With less than two months behind me as a separated woman, nights were no longer spent crying and cursing Derrick. I actually slept through a few of them now.

There was no way in hell to miss daybreak since my bay window was its resting place. At first light of day, my eyes popped open and my nose twinkled at the smell of fresh-brewed coffee and something fried. Regina was already up and dressed for fishing. I still couldn't believe she was the one who picked Alaska. I looked down the steps at her sitting at the huge Waltons-size table, sipping piping hot coffee and glancing at the stove every few seconds as some kind of meat lay frying in a pan.

"Morning girl. Bacon. Figured we'd need something to stick to our ribs since we're gonna be out bonding with nature all day," Regina chanted as I stumbled down the steps with outstretched hands, begging for coffee.

"Lying under the hot sun, cabana boys at my beck and call. Did none of those things cross your mind when you were planning a vacation for me? We can't meet men up here at the North Pole."

"Spoken just like a woman who's never been stripped naked

and ravaged by a man who hunts bear for a hobby," she smiled, turning bacon in the hot frying pan.

Karen walked in during the stripped-naked comment and didn't dare ask what we were talking about. Somehow being stripped naked in Alaska temperatures didn't appeal to her, either. We all gobbled down bacon, eggs, toast, and several cups of coffee before the knock at the door. It was Percy, our over-sixty-five-year-old fishing guide.

Although we had a boat of our own, we decided to rent one of the guided boats. None of us had ever spent more than a few seconds in a boat, so it was in our life's interest that we seek help. Percy hobbled in, handing out rubber pants that were clearly made to fit a three-hundred-pound man.

"Put these on, girls. Water's cold this time of year. It's damn cold year round, but plenty cold this time of year," he laughed, and we all followed suit.

As I slid the rubbers over my jeans I kept an eye on Percy, who wasn't wearing anything rubber except green boots with thick brown soles covered in as much thick brown mud. His pants were standard blue cotton work pants. I imagined at least two or three pair of thermal underwear underneath. His red (and all the other colors of the rainbow) plaid shirt hung over his pants. The ensemble was topped off with a camouflage ball cap that matched nothing else on his person. He strutted around the chalet like this was common ground for him. After we all had our clown pants on, he opened the door for us and started talking to the air surrounding him, not bothering to make eye contact with either of us.

Equipped with rods, reels, bait, tackle, a jet boat, and Percy, we were ready for fishing in the Little Sustina River. Since we were trying to see as much of the area as possible, we chose to go almost an hour away to Little Su, as Percy called it, to try our hand at silver salmon fishing.

As we piled into Percy's pickup truck, I glanced back at the boat. Knowing nothing about boats or fishing, I rested assured in the fact that it looked like other boats I had seen in my thirty-three years in Jacksonville. It looked large enough for the four of us, but no more. There were coolers on both sides of the boat. I smiled at the likelihood that we would need even one cooler.

Karen got shoved right up against Percy, with Regina in the middle and me trying to get enough of my butt in the vehicle so I could close the door. The rubber pants made that feat more difficult and the hour-long drive a hot, stuffy one. Not like the cold ride from the day before.

"That's the flatlands," Percy said, pointing out to a marshy-looking area that went on forever. Patches of green and brown grass and weeds broken up by spots of deep blue water. My mind drifted back to the city we drove through from the airport. The tall office buildings and the Ruby Tuesday restaurant I had made a mental note about, as I pouted about the unexpected vacation. That city could have been a million miles away from the serene place Percy's truck was pushing through. A noise overhead yanked my head up as my eyes fell on a flock of geese soaring just above the flatlands. I felt like an outsider in this place that was so unspoiled by human hands.

I looked over at Percy, who was chatting with Karen and Regina. He was unspoiled, too. His rough, calloused hands barely touched the steering wheel as he pointed and instructed. The speedometer was barely tagging thirty-five, as Percy seemed more interested in conversation than driving. Karen and Regina listened and turned their heads left and right as he gave the lay of the land. I was too far behind to catch up to their chatter, so I tilted my head back toward the window, out over the flatlands, and whispered a prayer that I would one day feel as at home and free in my own skin as Percy was in his aged, spotted layers of epidermis. I opened my eyes, mouthed an amen, and let myself drift about slowly in this place so far removed from all the hurt and pain that had taken up residence in my life.

By the time we reached our spot along the Little Su, I was looking forward to the boat, the water, and trying my hand at fishing. I opened the door of the pickup, my right leg flew out, and my foot landed on the cold, wet pavement. As I slid from the seat and adjusted my rubber pants, a tear fell from my eye as I allowed the simple act to take on a much higher meaning. A symbol of my first step in breaking free from the box that for so many years had been my safety net, my prison.

Within no time Percy, who could have easily been our grand-father, made us all comfortable enough to get into the boat, take a line in hand, and attempt to do something close to fishing. We spent about two and a half hours traipsing along Little Su watching Percy catch fish and make us think we had done it. Karen warned us that we'd have to catch something since this was going to be dinner. I didn't complain; I love fresh fish and especially a good salmon, but my mind drifted on to the hunting day. What would we have to kill in order to have dinner that day?

With three decent-size salmon in the cooler, Percy assured us that we had done better than most of the men that take the tour, so that was all we needed to know. We beat the average man. Mission accomplished.

Percy took the salmon to a station near the chalet to have them cleaned and filleted. We waited in his truck and had too many interesting jokes about his overt flirting with Karen. Karen was skilled and flirted back just enough to get Percy to drop the $185 guide fee he normally charges. He said it was because we didn't stay out long, but we knew it had more to do with Karen's erect nipples poking through her t-shirt when the wind blew enough to chill her. Percy even pulled out a Polaroid and snapped a shot of the three of us kneeling over the fish. He took two shots, one for us and one for his private pin-up collection of "chilly nipples."

With filleted salmon and tired achy bodies, we headed back to the chalet. While Karen marinated the salmon, Regina and I hit the sauna. Karen wasn't far behind, and by 6:00 on our first full day in Alaska, we were living the life. Salmon fresh from the Little Su and hot steam piercing the aches that surprised all three of us.

I put in a quick call to Mama after Karen was done talking to Randy. Sure enough, Derrick had picked the boys up first thing that morning and dropped them off at school. They were supposed to get pizza for dinner and then go to the game. He was going to keep them a second night since the game wouldn't be over until late and he didn't want to drive all the way back to Mama's house. As she talked, my mind lingered on the fact that my boys were staying at his girlfriend's house for two nights. Derrick and Minnie were a regular item now and I tried to picture her interacting with the boys. She was tall and thin and attractive to look at. Jealousy swelled in my throat as Mama went on talking about the warm front that had come in. I wondered if the boys liked Minnie and what they called her. Even if Derrick married that whore, those boys would never call her mama. I made a mental note to talk to them about that when I got back home.

Since everyone was done checking on things at home, we dragged our achy bodies into the sauna for steamy sex talk that would make a prostitute blush. The usual stuff, until Regina took things in a strange direction.

"You ever thought about what it would be like with another woman?" she asked, as sweat poured down our aching bodies.

Karen's eyelids slid open and I think I stopped breathing for a few seconds.

"Another woman," Karen said, as if begging Regina to clarify.

"Yes, like you know, lesbian stuff," Regina said, and I saw my chest rise and fall again.

"Well, with everything I've been through, I'm not sure either sex is an option. I just want some by-myself time," I interjected, realizing Regina was simply making small talk.

Karen didn't seem so convinced.

"I'm quite satisfied with what I have. Why do you ask, Regina?" she added, sitting forward on the sauna bench with a grave expression running across her face.

"Oh Lord, girl, why do you have to make such a production of everything? You know what I mean. You never thought about messing around with one of those little cuties back when you were in college? I know you white girls," Regina said, tossing in her own unique form of racial slur.

I let the giggle trickle from my lips as Karen took offense at the remark and then blew it off. She sat back against the wall, and closed her eyes again.

"No, not really. I mean, some of the girls in the dorm did things, but I was never interested," Karen ended, not bothering to open her eyes.

"And you?" I felt the need to ask, since Regina had gone there.

"Well, now that you mention it, there is this girl at work," she said and then paused.

I felt my breathing stop again. Karen's eyelids didn't pop open this time. I started back breathing. Karen wasn't taking her seriously, so I chose that path as well.

"Yeah, right. This from the woman who changes men more often than J-Lo," I said, letting Regina off the hook.

We all had a good laugh and continued bad mouthing J-Lo for at least another fifteen minutes or so. After nearly an hour of relaxation, we were ready for dinner. Karen and Regina had agreed to take turns with the meals, and even though it was Karen's turn, Regina insisted on cooking. She baked the salmon, tossed the canned veggies into a pot, and in no time dinner was served. The three of us spread out around the table like the twelve disciples and broke bread like we hadn't eaten in days. The conversation veered from serious girl cry talk, to all men are dogs, to the infamous why men think clitoris is just a myth. By midnight, I couldn't imagine any place I'd rather be than Alaska, with my girls.

22

Our third day was set aside for hunting. The mere thought of the word made me laugh. As if any of us would actually kill an animal. The morning started a bit different from our fishing morning in that we were required to be out before dawn. That meant half asleep and cold-as-ice temperatures. As I dragged my lazy behind out the door to load the truck with Jeff the hunting guide, I thought about backing out.

Jeff was a good deal younger than Percy, closer to our age. He was wearing full camouflage gear and the same kind of nasty rubber boots as Percy. They looked like they had trudged through the same mud hole. Jeff's red hair poked out the sides of his ball cap and his freckled face, complete with blank stare, added to his look to create exactly what I imagined in a hunting guide.

It was dark and cold, and Jeff made it known by his stomping and slamming that he wasn't in a good mood. He must have lost the hunting guide's bet last night since he got stuck with the women. Karen let Jeff know right out of the gate that we had no intention of killing any animals. Jeff seemed even more delighted to get this bit of news.

"We simply want to learn the art of hunting. The do's and don'ts and how to conduct yourself safely in the wild with other hunters," Karen rattled off as if she were the guide instead of Jeff.

Jeff stared into the dark, growing more impatient with Karen's speech. He didn't seem the least bit impressed by her breasts or anything else. No discounted rates on this one, I thought, as Jeff led the way out the front door of the chalet.

"We need to get going, sun'll be up after while and won't be any need of going out then. We need to already be out there when day breaks. That's rule number one, I guess," he added, trying to stick with Karen's lesson plan.

We loaded the truck and of course I got stuck sitting beside the rifles, a huge bow and arrow, and something that looked like explosives. I wondered why we needed so much stuff just to learn the basics of hunting. Perhaps Jeff actually thought he might get to kill something; oh what a surprise he was in for. If he so much as frightened one of the animals, Karen would be all over him like ugly on a monkey. I sat in the back laughing at my own madness, as Jeff paid no attention to the bumps in the unpaved road that led to the depths of nowhere. He, unlike Percy, was pushing the little black marker on the speedometer close to sixty.

Jeff explained the "fair chase, leave no trace," method of hunting as we bumped along. I glanced at the guns occasionally, wondering if they were loaded and if the knocking about of the rough ride might make one of them go off, shoot me in the head, leave me dead, and turn my vacation into a funeral. Jeff babbled on about the importance of leaving the woods in the same state we found it, not disturbing nature and all that crap. I think piercing a hole in an animal with a tiny bullet and then watching the life drain from its body is going slightly beyond disturbing the natural environment. But it was not my place to speak, only listen and learn, and try to stay awake.

By the time we got to some specific place in the woods, we started unloading gear. Jeff assured us that all the weapons were unloaded and safe to handle, but at all times we were to keep the rifles aimed upward to the sky and not at an unsuspecting friend.

"Pointing a gun, loaded or unloaded, is a good way to end a

friendship," Jeff joked, and we all laughed at his attempt to lighten the mood.

After we all had rifles in hand and packs around our waists with supplies, Jeff started the trek further into the woods. I thought we were in the woods, until we started the foot journey. There was no path, only trees and brush and vines hanging everywhere; it's a wonder the animals could get around in this place. Just as there was specific attire for fishing, there was equally attractive apparel for hunting. We all blended in nicely with the surroundings covered in camouflage everything.

Jeff ran down the list of animals we might see and the ones that were legal to hunt. Moose, black bear, wolf, coyote, red fox, lynx, and then your more tame animals like squirrel and rabbit. Jeff's list would have excited the normal hunter, but the list scared the daylights out of three women from Florida. Jeff had to turn around and look for us, as our steps slowed at each name on his list. Bears and wolves and foxes are not the things I was looking forward to seeing just at the break of day in the woods of Alaska. So if the rifle in the truck didn't go off and kill me, I would be mauled by a black bear as Jeff, Karen, and Regina tried to leave the forest undisturbed.

The next three to four hours were spent avoiding most of the animals Jeff mentioned, but we did manage to see several rabbits and squirrels. I thought I would pee my pants when suddenly Jeff stopped and threw his hand up for us to halt. There was silence, I could hear my heart pounding, and all I wanted was to stop it so whatever was ahead of us wouldn't hear it and commence to rip it out of my chest.

Jeff took another few steps ahead, but didn't have to tell us to stay still. He couldn't have paid us to move. He pulled back some branches to clear a line of sight through the woods just enough for us to see. He waved his hand for us to step closer. He waved a second time, since still none of us moved. We all stepped in unison toward Jeff's motion. And there in the clearing just fifteen feet away was a moose minding his business completely unaware that we were there. We all wanted it to stay that way, so Jeff let the branches fall back into place slowly and led us in another direction away from the animal. When we were far enough away to talk, he told us that we were going to head back out the way we came in, since the mama moose was not far from her baby, and we all agreed we had no desire to run into mama.

Within no time, we were back at the truck eagerly loading rifles and those things that were around our waist back into Jeff's pickup truck. I had had about as much as I could stand of Mother Nature for two days. I wanted a hot shower and some food I didn't have to kill first.

23

We grabbed lunch at the same diner from our first day. This time we were the only ones in the place besides Emily and Daniel. I kind of felt deprived as we walked in and didn't see the warm smiles we left two days earlier. Emily made small talk and brought us big helpings of vegetables. After wandering around in the woods with the creatures, there was no way I wanted to eat one. A feeling I was certain would pass after I got the pictures of baby moose out of my head.

With lunch leftovers in hand, we went back to the chalet for naps and the occasional Jeff the hunter jokes. Regina was convinced he would be a hoot in bed. Karen was just afraid of him because he seemed to know the woods a little too well, and I couldn't even pick him out in a crowd if I ever saw him again. There was nothing about Jeff that struck my fancy, but it was entertaining to hear Regina and Karen describe what sounded like two completely different men.

After our naps, we woke up just in time to gobble down the lunch leftovers and catch the sunset. Might I mention that it was past nine o'clock at night? We got to experience some of the longest days, nearly seventeen hours of daylight. So it was clear that our internal clocks were off a little since there didn't seem to be much time for night sleeping.

At sunset, the next logical thing was a come-to-Jessi session. We had spent half of our vacation without mention of him, but I knew it would come up sooner or later. And of course Regina went there.

"You heard from that fool lately?"

"Regina . . ." Karen scolded.

"It's okay. I was waiting for his name to come up." I paused, having wanted the conversation but now not knowing where to go with it.

"No, I haven't heard from him and I don't expect to. He's moved on and with any luck, I'll do the same. He picked the boys up yesterday. Took them to a football game. As long as he does for them, I'm okay."

"You certainly will be okay. Jessi girl, you can do whatever you set your mind to," Regina added.

"Yeah, Jess, and I know you think it's crazy, but maybe you should do something like start your own business," Karen interjected like it wasn't the huge joke I took it for.

"My own business, and what in the world do you think I could do, or sell, for that matter?"

"Shoes, and some of them damn pocketbooks," Regina jumped in without invitation.

We all laughed at the memory of Reginald and Randy carrying boxes and boxes of shoes and handbags out of the house on packing day. Regina said it as a joke, but it was just what Karen needed to get her juices flowing.

"She may have something there, Jess. Nobody knows more about shoes and bags than you. You would buy the latest Weitzman if it meant giving up food."

She was right about that. Not that I'd given up food. I'd just bought plenty of both.

"But a business. You all may not know, but I for one know all the pitfalls of new startups with clever ideas of breaking into an existing market, and after months of empty stores and stagnant stock they shut down. I see it every day in my line of work," I said, not really wanting to end the conversation.

It was refreshing to focus on something that I really knew a good deal about. Even if the idea was far-fetched, it felt good to talk about it.

"All the more reason you could make it work. You already know the pitfalls. You're a step ahead of most people already," Karen added, as if sensing my desire to go on.

I sat and listened to the girls chug coffee and plan my business venture. Regina had me selling shoes and bags out of some kind of mobile Fashion on Wheels truck, and Karen had me taking up a space the size of Jewelry Shack at the mall. Although both were equally ridiculous, the thought of my own business did sound kind of nice. But who was gonna buy anything from a thirty-three-year-old, divorced, overweight black woman with a master's degree she got taking Internet courses? Little did I know my friends had plans to deal with some of my other problems as well.

"And you'll need to drop a pound or two. Research shows heavier women earn as much as fifty percent less than slimmer people," Regina threw in without regard for my already fragile state.

"Regina . . ." Karen chided again.

I would have rather seen Karen slap her face. That was what I wanted to do, but then again, Regina was stronger than both of us, and physical confrontation wasn't a thing I wanted to risk. It's not exactly what you want from your vacation.

After a long pause, I was sure that this conversation was over and had ended on an awkward note, but there was no stopping Regina once she was onto something. And she was indeed onto something. I too had seen the research about obesity and pay rates. I had read that same article and then sat my container of chocolate almond Häagen-Dazs right on top of it.

"It's fall now, so the temps are cool enough to do some stuff outside, like walking. I'd start simple, nothing to shock your body too much. And exercise does no good without decent eating habits," Regina added, crossing one of her rippling quadriceps across the other.

I immediately looked away from the sight. Karen was petite and her body mostly the result of genetics, but Regina was big

boned, and her tight body the result of hours in the gym. If anyone had a right to talk about getting fit, it was her, since she
worked so hard at it. But that didn't matter. Even if she had
been workout guru Billy Blanks, I didn't want to hear this, not
now anyway. I didn't bother to make eye contact with either of
them. I looked down at my feet, and the walls around us. Silence
is usually a good sign that this line of discussion should end, but
Regina didn't seem to be following my lead.

"Don't you agree?" she said, slapping her hand toward Karen.

Karen didn't answer. Her expression looked like a cross between fear and constipation. She looked at me as if wanting to
provide a rock for me to crawl under. By now, they had my attention. I silently prayed for the strength to help me get through
this conversation.

After a few seconds of silence, if for no other reason than to
get her to finish her subtle attack and shut the hell up about my
fat ass and walking, I focused on Regina and her rambling started
again. And the more I listened the more she talked. Karen chose
to relieve the tension by perking another pot of coffee, and that
was my signal that my makeover was just getting started. I prayed
again, this time for the strength not to do bodily harm to either
of my friends.

"Jess, you'd be surprised how much better you'd feel about
yourself if you ate better and took better care of yourself.
Regina does have a point. I just think she could approach it better," Karen added, dumping old coffee grinds into the trash.

"And who made you the Queen of Tact, missy?"

Then the two of them got into it, which gave me a respite
from hearing about how much I needed to change. Fact of the
matter, I was tired of people telling me I needed to change. Like
I wasn't good enough.

During my marriage it plagued me. Was Derrick checking
out other women because there was something wrong with me?
And now my own friends were putting it right out in front of
me. They too thought Jess wasn't good enough. Their bickering
was all I could take on such a cold night that should have been

enveloped in a dark blanket by now, but the Alaska sun didn't seem to know when to sit its ass down.

"I'm going to bed," I announced, as Karen and Regina finally noticed that I was still in the room.

"Are you okay?"

"I'm fine, just too fat and insecure for anymore of this shit."

I stormed up to the Good Room and was glad the sun hadn't gone down yet. It gave me a chance to catch a glimpse of the scene just outside my bedroom window. The scene that from day one we all described as beautiful, like the spot further down the lake where the trees slumped over, dimming it and making it look cold and dark, wasn't beautiful too. We always assign things. This is beautiful and that isn't. And not just things, but people. There is a standard definition of beautiful people, and I did not fit it. Beautiful people start businesses, have happy, satisfied husbands and fulfilled lives. The rest of us just watch them from a distant point down the river, wishing for their light, their brilliance.

The girls didn't bother to come in and console me. I was glad. I needed time to lick my wounds. So much had happened in the past month that the last thing I needed was to feel more inadequate. There was no denying my weight, hair, nails, and overall disposition needed an adjustment, but neither my heart nor pocketbook could take the weight of making all those changes. As the Alaska sun finally retired for the night, I lay awake, staring into the still darkness with only my true thoughts. My most honest feelings.

I did want things to be different. I didn't want the extra weight. It was only thirty pounds or so, but it was thirty pounds I didn't want. I've never let my hair go like this or not squeezed in a manicure just so my nails don't start to yellow and break off. And I'll be damned, I do know more about shoes and handbags than your average mortal, and my business degree is just as good as anyone else's. I could start my own thing, and even if it failed, at least it would be some direction for me when I returned to normal temperatures and days that only last ten or twelve hours at a time.

I sat up in the bed and proclaimed to myself that I wanted a change and I could make it all work. The business, the eating, and the exercise—even though the last one felt more like a dirty word than the rest. I stormed out of my bedroom to make my announcement to the others, but the hall was dark. The downstairs lights were out and when I looked at each room door, there was no light peering from under the large slabs of wood. They were asleep, as any sensible person should be at midnight in the frozen woods of Palmer.

I sat back down in my bed with pen and paper and sketched a plan. Everything from kicking the donut-and-Coke breakfast habit to joining Regina's gym. I even tossed in some ideas about a business. That part was the most far-fetched, but with a few lines on paper, it was coming into view and didn't look like a bad plan, for a thirty-three-year-old black woman with time and talent on her side.

24

When the sun rose the morning of day four, I wasn't so quick to jump out of bed. I could hear the girls downstairs yapping just like they were last night. I looked around the bed at the pieces of paper that had crumpled under my tossing and turning. They were the papers from the brochure Regina had with all the detail about the trip. I had scribbled my plans all over the back of every page. I looked over the things again in the light of day and tossed them aside before fear could slap me back into thinking I couldn't do it. I wasn't going to share any of it with the girls. This one wasn't about them, or anyone except Jessi. I needed to do this for me, and no one else.

As the papers fell to the backside of the bed, I noticed day four meant going to the camper. I had nearly forgotten that it was almost over. Just a few more hours and we would become one with the elements. The thought sent a chill, so I wrapped up in the blanket and dozed off again, listening to the giggling and talking that was once in the distance coming closer.

"We let you have your time last night, but I think you owe us the pleasure of your smiling face at the disciples' table," Karen proclaimed from the doorway of the Good Room.

I couldn't help but laugh and roll out of bed to join them in packing our things. We had set aside the day for repacking and getting ready for the move into the camper. The girls didn't mention my temper tantrum from the night before, just as I suspected they wouldn't. That's the way it is with friends. You can show your behind and they still love you.

With all our things packed and loaded we drove the car back toward the main house, and we were supposed to find the camper there ready to load and go. Sure enough, when we got to the main house, Mr. Monroe was there with hot cups of coffee and the keys to the camper. Another old white guy, I thought as I sipped the coffee and listened to Karen ask questions about the camper. Monroe looked more like a former New York businessman trying to fit into the great outdoors. At least fifty years old, he was wearing the same kind of blue work pants as Percy, but his look was more like "white-collar dress-down-day pants." His light blue polo button-down and the pen hung over his left ear added the final touches to his mailroom guy look.

With a few instructions, we were ready to load and go. Day five we were scheduled to do some touring, but for the remainder of this day we would just drive back to Anchorage and find a place to hunker down for the night. Monroe told us about a nightspot in town that might give us a chance to let our hair down and kick up our heels. I couldn't imagine what a nightclub in Alaska might be like, but my curiosity was getting the best of me. As we unloaded things from the car and loaded the camper, we decided to head to Anchorage and do a little dancing with the locals.

The camper was huge and Monroe had let us know it was Class A, which meant absolutely nothing to me, but once I got inside I was sure I never would want to travel in anything but Class A. It was much nicer than I ever imagined it would be. Just like the chalet, the camper surprised me, and I was more excited about spending a couple of days in a house on wheels. And then the crazy thought hit me, "Was Monroe his first or last name?" I didn't bother to ask.

Karen made her way to the driver's seat, knowing that would be her responsibility for the duration of the trip. It's amazing how friends who know each other so well know their place in the scheme of things. No one had to ask Karen to drive; she already knew she was the most responsible and mothering type. So no question, she was the driver.

I peeked at the driver's area just out of curiosity and it didn't look half bad. There was a huge dash panel equipped with everything I would imagine you'd need to drive something as monstrous as a house. There was even an in-dash monitor to show you the view from a camera mounted on the back of the vehicle. The perfect helper when trying to back this thing.

At first glance, the inside of the motor home looked nothing like I had imagined from the outside. My first question was how all that was inside this box on wheels. The driver's seat is a swivel recliner, so when Karen isn't driving she can swivel around and chill with the rest of us. The passenger-side seat is also a recliner, and if that's not enough reclining there is one more in the seating area. Across from the recliner in the seating area is a long couch with seating for at least four adults. The couch is also a full-size bed. The next section is the kitchen, equipped with plenty of cabinet space, an extra-large four-door refrigerator-freezer, stove with oven, deep-bowl double sink, microwave, and dining table for three. Just past the kitchen leading to the bedroom is the pantry and storage area. Yes, there is separate bedroom. The bedroom area is equipped with a queen-size bed, built-in entertainment center with twenty-five-inch television, a desk area, lots of drawers and storage space, and a bathroom. The bathroom has the separate commode room, neo-angle residential-size shower with overhead skylight, sink with storage below, and mirrored medicine cabinet above.

With all our things loaded into the camper, we set out for Anchorage. The two-hour drive gave Regina and me time to get all our things set up and put the food away. Regina was setting out her toiletries in the bathroom while I loaded my one of three drawers of the dresser/desk thingy beside the bed. We were still living on the basics we picked up from Daniel at the diner in Palmer the first day we got to town. Supplies were running low, but we were confident there would be a Wal-Mart or something large and commercial in Anchorage.

The drive also gave me time to log a call home. The boys had just come in from school and were eager to tell me all about the football game with their dad. I listened and sounded excited although I was secretly wishing they'd mention Minnie and say hateful, cruel things about her. But they didn't once mention anyone else except their dad, the game, and the jokes about me shooting a bear in Alaska. Mama took the phone after the boys were done with their dual report. By the time I heard her voice on the line, I was worn out from listening to two renditions of the same stories at the same time.

"Was she with him?" I asked Mama after getting her take on the night out with Daddy.

"Jessi, why you worrying about that? You all the way in Alaska, worrying about a man that doesn't even deserve the attention."

"That's quite a change in only a few short weeks, Mama," I sighed.

"I just wanted what was best for you. Took me too long to see what that was. And to answer you, no, I don't think she was with them. The boys didn't mention her."

With that admission, I felt better and free to enjoy a night on the town in Anchorage. I gave Mama the specifics of our return trip, so that they would meet us at the airport on time. And with that, the two-hour trip to Anchorage was behind us.

Karen asked for a few directions and quickly found the place to park the camper: a huge lot with lots of other campers and really big vehicles that shouldn't even be allowed on the road with normal cars. Karen joined us in the back to make plans for our night out in Anchorage. We hadn't really packed clothes for partying, but it didn't matter since we wouldn't likely ever see these people again. We'd wear whatever we could rustle up at Wal-Mart and dance our little mainland American rear ends off.

Karen ventured out to talk to the other campers about where all the hotspots were. Most of them were older white people, so Karen was the perfect choice to send out. Regina would have only frightened them. She still frightened me and I'd known her for nearly twenty years. Karen returned with all the details for the Wal-Mart trip and the hotspot for partying. She cranked that monster up again and headed out, in search of bargain shopping and some good times that didn't include killing wildlife.

Still no one mentioned the business idea or the diet they were eager to put me on. And no one mentioned Derrick. We had gone four days without any heated discussions about The Ex, which he was permanently referred to as. I thought about him often. Everything from hating his guts for putting me in this predicament, to hating his guts for moving on without so much as one stumbling block. I was certain he wasn't spending sleepless nights worrying about his weight or what direction his life was going to take now. He had that idiot Minnie, his car dealership, and those ignorant church people who didn't have the common sense required to see his sinful ways. The more we shopped and toured the sites of Anchorage, the more I hated him and the more I wanted the life Jessi should have had all along.

Anchorage had most of the modern conveniences of mainland United States. We found a steakhouse with plenty of red meat. So each of us ordered the biggest steaks they had, cooked our way. Regina well done, Karen rare, and me right in the middle.

"Girl, your steak is subject to jump right off the plate, you better get them to cook it some more." Regina glared at Karen as if we didn't go through this every time we went to dinner together.

"I know what I like. And besides, if the steak jumps off the plate, thanks to Jeff the hunting guide, I know how to catch it."

The two of them went on for a while longer with conflicting reports about the latest FDA findings about red meat. I tuned them out and watched the others in the restaurant. It was clear which folk were locals and which were tourists. In Anchorage the locals looked just like the downtown businessfolk in Jacksonville. Business casual was the order of the day. The tourists looked more like Percy knockoffs. Outdoorsy clothes and t-shirts with Alaskan slogans and pictures of moose and glaciers. I looked around our table at Regina and Karen yapping like hyenas and decided we indeed fit with the tourists look.

The steaks were cooked to order, and as soon as the waitress set them down and walked away, the conversation stopped. Three otherwise dignified women tore into the meat like it was the best thing we'd seen in days.

Emily, the waitress in Palmer, had suggested taking a tour or visiting the museum while we were in Anchorage. Turns out September is off-season for the Native Heritage Center, but the tour trolley was just pulling in for the next group, by the time we made our way to Fourth Avenue. With beef weighing heavy, we made our way from the largest and busiest floatplane base, to one of Alaska's many wild geese and duck sanctuaries. Several riders got off at certain points along the trail to spend extra time. With trolleys leaving every fifteen minutes, they could just catch the next one and continue with a new group. We chose to enjoy the one-hour journey from the same seat we boarded in downtown Anchorage.

From Point Woronzof, one of the stops on the tour, you could see a perfect view of downtown Anchorage. I closed my eyes and let my spirit bond with everything I had seen. Little Su, the dense woods, and now the city that is home to half of the state's six hundred thousand residents. The tall office buildings and occasional fast-food restaurants, although necessary for the growing population, seemed strangely out of place. Just outside the city limits is the Alaska of yesteryear. The frontier that beckoned to William Henry Seward, the secretary of state who worked to make Alaska a part of the United States. The trolley ride was a great opportunity to let our food digest, as well as a deeper message my soul was yearning for. Sometimes you have to step back and take a look from a distance, close your eyes and open your heart, to see the true beauty of a thing.

When we got back to the camper Karen was tired from all the mothering she had been doing all day. From driving the camper to helping us all find our way, to getting decent clothes for us to wear for a night out. She was tuckered out and retreated to the bedroom for a nap.

It was the perfect opportunity for me to pick Regina's brain. After so many years, I had never questioned their friendship. I always thought Karen and Regina were an odd pair, but I just accepted it and never gave it much thought as to how and why. Karen had given me her side of the story. Now it was Regina's turn.

"What's on your mind, lady?"

"Nothing much, just wondering about you two."

"Who two?"

"You and Karen, how you can fight so much and still be so close. And be so different and still accept each other?"

"Girl, you straining your brain about that. That's easy, Karen's scared shitless of me. She accepts me 'cause I'll beat her ass if she don't," she said and fell over laughing.

Regina hated to get into serious, deep conversations and she was avoiding this one in her usual fashion. Everything boiled down to kicking someone's ass. But she wasn't getting off the hook so easy.

"Seriously, what's the deal?"

"I don't know. We just keep it real, that's all."

"But you tried to kill her in high school. And you would've if you hadn't tripped over that pack."

"Yeah, well we worked it out. I didn't see Karen as one of us. So I didn't like the fact that she was with Randy. I figured she was just using him."

"What changed your mind?"

"I got to know her. I found out we were alike in the important stuff, and the stuff where we're different, we help each other."

Regina got a distant look in her eye and started with the story of how a tampon changed her relationship with Karen forever. The day of the peer mediation meeting, Regina had started her period at school and didn't have a maxi-pad. Her biggest fear was that the blood had seeped through her pink shorts, and sure enough, it had. Karen spotted her first and followed her to the bathroom before anyone else could see it. Karen then went to her locker, got her gym clothes out with fresh underwear and shorts . . . and a tampon. Regina didn't know how to use a tampon because her mother never got to go over that lesson with her before she died. Her aunt that got custody of her was a prude who shrieked at the thought of anything being stuck into her vagina, so she started Regina on pads when she first got her period. Not only did Karen spare her embarrassment, give her fresh clothes and sanitary protection, she taught her how to use it.

"Girl, when you learn how to do something as personal as put on a tampon with someone, it creates a bond. Karen never made a big deal out of it, but I think it was a lesson both of us needed. We all bleed red blood, and we all have feelings."

Regina finished her tampon story, pushed her rear forward to recline the chair, laid back, and closed her eyes. So that was the story behind it. A surprise period and a tampon created a friendship that has lasted nearly twenty years. No wonder they never tell anyone why they're such good friends.

25

Against my better judgment, I let Regina pick out my clothes for the nightclub. A short-sleeve, silk, lime green blouse she'd picked up at the Wal-Mart was far too tight and low-cut. I was shoving too much cleavage at the well-meaning Alaskan men and women, but at least I had on a pair of decent shoes. My only pair of Manolos. The ones I had hid in the back of the closet for nearly a year because I was too embarrassed at how much I'd paid for them.

Karen was modestly dressed in a cute navy blue dress that screamed "married woman," and as usual, Regina was down-right outrageous. Her miniskirt, which was one of many, gave full view of those tight legs that I had been trying to ignore since our weight-loss talk. And her strapless sequin blouse would have fit in perfect at someplace tropical. In Alaska, it made us look more like extremely horny tourists.

We rested until 9:00 p.m. and then made our way to Pier 66. It looked like your typical nightspot from the outside, but the name had me concerned. I wasn't sure if we'd find more people dressed like Percy and Jeff inside. We walked through the double doors and a man with a huge smile welcomed us with a nod and an open hand. He was reaching for the five-dollar cover charge, but Karen gave the hand a nice shake before realizing that.

There was a band in one of the corners, a bar in the other, and tables around the perimeters of a large wood slab covered with swaying couples. I didn't recognize any of the music. We got the same type of stares we did our first day in Palmer. A room full of older white women and men swung their heads around in unison as we made our way toward an empty table. We took our seats and a few people held their gaze, but for the most part everyone smiled and went back to their drinking, talking, and dancing.

"I'm gonna need a stiff one to get through this," Regina announced on her way to the bar.

Karen and I followed, not sure what else to do. We all got drinks and resumed our position at the small table with four chairs in the corner. The table was so small the three drinks took up most of the space, so we sat our purses on the floor. I scanned the room again as if I would see something different this time. But still just a room full of older white men and women. Most of them were modestly dressed in skirts and blouses and button-down shirts for the men. We were clearly overdressed, but that was the least of the reasons we stood out. With my head still I let my eyes scale the room, careful not to spend too much time looking at any one thing. Five couples on the dance floor that at closer inspection was definitely a series of big wood slabs held together by nails that were still protruding. I looked away, hoping the only lady wearing high heels would step on a nail and shove it back down into the wood. Two swinging doors led to some other room. It reminded me of the *Gunsmoke* saloon doors. There were two men standing at the bar waiting for drinks and making small talk. The bar looked more like a series of two-by-fours nailed together and painted brown, no nails protruding. There was a neon sign overhead that read BAR. Clever, I thought, as I let my eyes keep moving. Three of the other eight tables were taken by groups of three or four . . . also older white people. I sighed, agreeing with Regina's comment about needing a stiff one. I started to sip my martini when out of nowhere a tall dark figure stepped through the swinging doors. The first black person we had seen since we got to Alaska. He took his place behind the bar, pulled an apron over his head and started wiping the counter and shifting bowls of nuts and pretzels. I hadn't seen another black face in so long, I couldn't seem to look away from his. And that's how he caught me checking him out.

"Karen and I are gonna dance and mingle a little, are you game?" Regina asked, with perfect timing since I needed some reason to look away from the lone black ranger.

"No, you go ahead. I'll hold our table."

Karen and Regina walked toward the middle of the dance floor and started swaying mildly to the sounds of Neil Diamond. It's amazing, I thought. Women can do that. Women can dance together and no one thinks a thing of it. People think it's cute, in fact. But let two men dance anywhere close to each other and they have to be gay. Amazing how it works, I thought as I watched them sway offbeat and giggle.

I looked back toward the bar, and this time I caught him staring at me. He looked away quickly just like you're supposed to. I looked back again to make sure. He looked again, too. It all felt so childish I had to smile. He smiled, too.

He wasn't attractive by most standards. Probably over fifty years old, with just a hint of gray around the edges of his mini-afro, and there was something very homely and plain about him. I couldn't for the life of me figure out why I kept looking at him and why the devil I smiled. I was sure he took it the wrong way when he started making his way toward my table.

"Can I get you another?" he asked, pointing toward my drink.

"Sure, that'd be great," I smiled again.

"My name is Sam. Sam Walston. What brings you to these parts?"

"You assume I'm not from these parts," I returned, batting my eyes like some silly fool, knowing full well I was not interested in talking to this man.

"You just don't have the look. You don't look like the cold-weather type."

"I'm not, as a matter of fact. I'm from Florida. Jessica Andrews, but my friends call me Jessi," I said, extending my hand toward his.

I was trying not to flirt, but the harder I tried, the more I flirted. Sam made himself at home until his partner at the bar motioned for him.

"Well, Jessi, won't you join me at the bar? My break is over and I'd like to know what brings a woman from the warmth of Florida to this chilly land."

Sam picked up my drink and carried it to the bar. I followed his tall, lean frame as if I didn't have a choice. I glanced at Regina as I took a seat in front of him at the bar. She winked and gave me that "you go girl" look. Karen was smiling and pulling her hands together like she was going to clap. Those fools, I thought, as I turned my attention back to Sam.

I made no mistake of leading Sam to think that I was anything more than a nice tourist on vacation from the mainland. I told him about my separation and about catching Derrick cheating. I also told him how much I thought I was going to hate this trip, but how in fact it had gone very well. Sam listened as I babbled. He kept my drink topped off and ventured away from me only for brief seconds to attend to the needs of the other two or three people at the bar. I glanced at Regina and Karen again, and they had gone back to the table and seemed in the middle of some kind of heated debate. I thought about the tampon story, smiled and went back to chatting with Sam.

At midnight, things were slowing down at the club, as if they weren't already dragging. I thought I saw Regina nod off once or twice. One old guy was hitting on Karen and her irritated expression let me know it was time to wrap up my conversation with Sam. I made pleasantries and left the bar to rescue my two friends. Karen was having no luck getting oldie to back off, so by the time I got to the table, Regina had taken matters into her own capable hands.

"Listen old man. This woman is married to a fine black man

back in Florida. That's right, black, and fine, damn fine. He's half your age and twice your size if you get my drift, so I suggest you step off, which in Alaskan means, GO AWAY."

Red faced and pissed off, the old guy mumbled some words under his breath, not daring to cross Regina. He looked at Karen and then at me before heading out the door. The scene gave us all a good laugh, which was short-lived since the only thing they wanted to know is whether or not I was going to be getting a piece before we left the frozen tundra.

Back at the camper, we sipped hot cocoa and recounted bits and pieces of the trip so far. The fishing guide staring at Karen's nipples, the hunting guide Regina wanted to get into bed, and me flirting my behind off with Sam. It felt good to feel attractive. I wasn't flirting with Sam because I was interested in him. He was older and revealed through our conversation that he was still in love with his deceased wife. That's how he got to Alaska. Her people were from Anchorage, so when she found out she was sick, he moved her back home. She lived six months longer than the doctors had given her. She had been dead five years and Sam still couldn't seem to leave Alaska and head back to warmer terrain. The girls thought Sam and I were making a love connection, but we were simply giving each other what we needed. I needed the attention and he needed to feel like he was turning the head of a younger woman. He was trying to get his life back into gear; perhaps spending four hours watching my batting eyes and pouting breasts spilling from my blouse was what he needed. He had certainly given me what I needed.

The girls turned in long before I did. This time I was not kept awake by the Derrick demons. Instead it was a burning in my gut. An anticipation of what I had to look forward to. Since that dreadful day, I had been focusing on everything that was wrong. I had spent years living in the shadow of Derrick and his business and music aspirations. For the first time, I was free to make my own choices. Free to do or not to do. As the distant howling of coyotes filled the night air, I drifted off to sleep drunk with the thought of a future full of possibility.

*   *   *

Our final day of the trip started with a glacier tour. All the touristy people loaded the huge boat and sailed out to an area close to, but not too close to the glaciers. The sight was beautiful, but it was cold. A bone-chilling cold that froze my fears and apprehensions. Surrounding the glacier were ice chunks not quite big enough to be icebergs.

"The largest one in the state is Mendenhall over in Juneau," the peppy tour guide informed us.

"This looks pretty big to me," I answered, as other tourists nodded in agreement.

"Yeah, but they're all shrinking. With global warming and all. Snowfall is the biggest factor for adding mass to a glacier, but that's not beating the warming nowadays," he returned.

The glacier ice is a dense Aqua Velva blue. The wind blowing across is fierce and cold and causes chunks to crack and pop, as they break apart.

"One good Alaskan glacier has more snow in it than all the glaciers in Switzerland," the guide added.

Some of the other tourists nodded with mouths turned up at the corners as if they were impressed by the statement. I figured they had visited Switzerland glaciers or just had an unnatural obsession for glacier facts and figures. By the time our tour was over, my body had taken all the cold it could handle and my mind was jam-packed with glacier knowledge. In Alaska, the glaciers are known as architects. They carve, chisel, and pulverize anything in their path. These huge masses advance and retreat in the ever-changing climate of Alaska.

When we got back to the camper and started packing our things, I noticed a note on the door. It was from Sam. Regina made comments and started singing that little childish song about Jessi and Sam sitting in a tree, k-i-s-s-i-n-g. Karen was too cold to tease, so she just laughed at Regina mocking six-year-olds with her singing. The note was short, but it confirmed what I thought. Sam appreciated the attention. He admitted that having a woman fifteen years his junior flirt with him gave him the motivation to take the next step. He had called relatives in Maryland and was considering moving back to the mainland.

I tucked the note away in my bag as I packed for the return trip home. In the freezing temperatures of Alaska, my heart was flooded with a warmth that would have melted that glacier.

26

When our plane landed at the Jacksonville Airport, both Randy and Reginald were waiting at the front gate. I watched the couples hug and express their happiness about being back at home. I didn't feel the same excitement. Not just because I hadn't found the three people who were supposed to be waiting for me, but because on a larger scale, I wasn't sure what was waiting for me.

Would the next year be filled with lonely nights fighting off depression and poverty, or would I meet a hotty and get swept off to never-never-land? I hugged Randy and Reginald out of courtesy. It's always awkward when you're the fifth wheel. Randy had glanced at me standing there not being embraced by anyone, so he loosened his grip on Karen long enough to try to make me feel welcome. It just felt awkward. Reginald followed suit and made it feel more weird. I wanted to tell them it wasn't necessary, but their hearts were in the right place. The guys grabbed things and we made our way out of the airport front gate. Karen and Regina were babbling in unison as Randy and Reginald listened with eager expressions.

I tried to hold my smile, still having no one to share the excitement with. But before I could sink to deep in despair, two handsome men dressed in blue jeans and Jacksonville Jaguar t-shirts attacked me. Everyone stood back as I wobbled and tried to keep my balance. The boys groped and hugged and talked as if I had been gone for months. Mama stood back with the others, watching us carrying on like crazy people. And for a moment, right there in the airport terminal, we were, and we didn't care who saw it.

I watched the others drive off as I got into Mama's car, still listening to endless stories from Josh and Jared. Since it was the weekend, I had agreed to stay at Mama's with the boys, just on a trial basis. She was still insisting that I move in with her, instead of being cramped at Regina's. I was apprehensive, but warming to the prospect. As Mama drove out of the parking lot, I sat in the front seat nodding my head toward the boys as if the words were registering. It didn't matter what they were saying, just that we were together and for the first time in a long time, it felt like it was going to be all right.

We drove past the patch of palms at the front of the airport. I noticed the sign at the gate. "Welcome To Jacksonville; Super Bowl 34 and Home of the PGA Tour." Welcome home, I thought, as the sign faded into the distance.

Within a few days everything was back to normal. Or normal since the hurricane. The weekend went well, so I made it official. The boys and I moved in with Mama. I had taken an extra day off work to see them off since they were headed to their new school. Mama was standing on the front porch waving and yelling out instructions to eight-year-olds who were doing everything except listening. With her in control of things with the boys, I decided to make the day productive and check into this business option we'd hammered away at during our vacation.

When the girls first mentioned starting my own shoe and handbag company, I thought it was just a neat idea and nothing more. The more thought I gave it, the more I wanted to check it out. Both Karen and Regina committed to back me financially if I decided to go for it, but there is no way I would waste their money or my own by doing something without all the necessary research and planning. So I started at the most logical place, the Small Business Center in Jacksonville.

From that first day I walked in, they treated me like royalty. I told them what my idea was and they led me to all the resources to use to find out if the plan was viable. My first step was to sign up for the TRAC program, which stands for training, resources, assessment services, and counseling. I registered for the program and got the schedule for the next nine-week set of classes that would go over everything from identifying potential problems to getting money to start the thing. When I left the center with both hands full of paperwork and materials, I was pumped about the possibility of doing what I've always loved; surrounding myself with shoes and handbags and being paid for it.

I left the center and, instead of going to work, I went straight to Karen's house. I walked in, stepping over toys and shoving baby bottles and bowls from the table. I spread out all the papers and gave her the five-minute version of the two hours I spent at the Small Business Center. By the time I was done, Kayla was screaming for a bottle and Karen was pulling out her checkbook. If I thought things were happening fast, they just got going faster as Karen wrote me a check for ten thousand dollars.

"Randy and I already talked about this and since you sound like you're gonna go for it, no sense in letting start-up capital stand in your way. Go on over and get Regina's share. She promised to help too, you know."

"Karen, this is too much. I can't let you guys do this. I'll have to pay you back," I insisted.

"No you will not, and if you don't take this money now, I'm coming into your shop when you open it and buy ten thousand dollars' worth of shoes and pocketbooks, so don't make me do that because I don't even carry a purse most of the time. Take the damn money and go on over to Regina's so I can feed my baby."

I gathered my papers as Karen heated up a bottle and stuck it into baby's mouth. Since I didn't know what else to do, I did as I was told. I went to Regina's place and spread out all the papers to start going over what I needed to do first. Working in the business world for more than ten years, and having a masters in business administration, I could have taught the guys at the center a thing or two. When Regina got home I was working on the business plan and already on-line pulling together information for the feasibility study.

"Didn't expect to see you. Hope you cooked something since you're here," she said, yanking the refrigerator door.

"No, I'm starting my own business, so I don't really have time to cook your meals."

"Girl, you gonna do it?" she screamed.

"Yep, and Karen and Randy wrote me a check for ten thousand, can you believe that?"

She didn't answer. She grabbed her purse with tears in her eyes and started writing her check. She too wrote a check for ten thousand.

"Regina, this is crazy," I insisted, looking at the check and then tossing it back down on the coffee table.

"It's my little nest egg. All I have in savings," she said, and reached for a box of tissues.

"Then I know this is crazy. I can't let you do this. Karen and Randy are always tossing money around, but you're a single woman. You need to hang on to this," I insisted.

"Stop being so bullheaded Jess. I really need to do this. This isn't all about you, you know."

I wasn't sure what to say to her. But I understood her sentiment completely. I reached down and picked up the check. The numbers and words on it blurred as I let myself feel the power of friendship.

"At least let me pay you back once the business is up and running," I begged, choking on the words.

"Oh you'll pay me back all right. Don't worry about that one bit. I don't ever plan to pay for another pair of shoes or pocketbook as long as I live."

With that the deal was done. I left Regina's place feeling like not only could I get a business off the ground, but I could make it soar. I came to a realization that they had obviously had all along. There's more to Jessica Andrews than meets the eye.

27

The Small Business Center set me up in their Adopt a Business program on level one, which is specially designed for people just starting a new business. They teach you how to get your license, how to work the legal structure of businesses, and more than you'd ever care to know about zoning law. I finished level one in no time and went straight to level two, which is fine-tuning the business plan, marketing, sales, and promotion and accounting information. By the time I finished level two, I was ready to go to the bank with my plan. I had watched so many other small businesses do these same things, and now I was doing them for myself.

Karen had been so bogged down with the kids and getting things back in order around her house, we hadn't spent any time together. Not even phone calls. I decided to change that and insisted we have lunch downtown on the river so I could tell her about my business plan.

We were scheduled to meet on the top deck of the landing. Karen was apparently running behind, so I took a seat at one of the tables and watched businessmen and -women darting off in all directions grabbing lunch, running errands, or just stepping outside to get a breath of fresh air. The upstairs area of the landing is a semicircle of white bistro tables and wrought-iron chairs. Upside-down-teardrop-shaped lighting fixtures lined the area. The teardrops were perched upon green leafy iron poles. The sun was warm beaming down on my head, so I looked up to see what was covering the area, or not covering it. There were wooden slabs laid in a crisscross pattern to let the sunlight shine through. Just enough to say there was a roof, but not enough to really protect you from the sun or rain.

I walked to the edge of the balcony area and looked down around the water fountain to see if I could spot Karen. I noticed a sign that read "Growth of a River City." I smiled, only hoping my business would be part of that growth. I looked across the St. John to the other side of the downtown area where the skyline was trimmed in tall rectangular-shaped buildings. Banks, offices, and the Prudential building were jutting into the air as if they wanted to go on forever. "A piece of the rock." With any luck I would soon get my piece, I thought, as I scanned the buildings and then looked back down toward the fountain in hopes of seeing Karen.

The tap on my shoulder was a welcome one. Karen had a big smile on her face and Kayla on her hip.

"Hey girl, I was just looking down for you. Nice day."

"Sure is. How did it go with the Small Business people?" Karen asked, shifting Kayla from one hip to the other.

I wondered why she didn't just put the little girl down. She could walk on her own, so it didn't make sense to me to stand there struggling to hold her.

"Let's grab a table before you topple over."

"Yeah, this girl is a handful, can't put her down. As soon as her feet hit the ground, she's off and running."

"I remember those days. Boys, times two. Climbing and yanking on everything in their path."

We took a seat as I noticed Kayla's hair all over her head looking springy and unkempt. I wasn't about to mention any-thing to Karen. She tried her best with that baby's hair, but how is a white girl gonna learn how to handle hair with that much kink in it? Karen was getting Kayla settled in the high chair while I surveyed the two. Did Karen ever feel self-conscious when she was out with her kids? They obviously had a black father. Did she ever wonder what people thought of her when they saw her dragging along two mixed kids? That would have been the kind of thing that I would think about. What other people are thinking when they look at me. That's part of my problem. Too concerned with what other people have to say and not concerned enough with what I want.

"Do you think you could help me do something with her hair?" Karen asked, as if she were reading my thoughts.

I didn't dare let on that I was sitting there wishing I could get a comb, a brush, and some hair grease on that child's hair.

"You need to get some hair grease first. It's awful dry."

"Grease? I thought the idea is to wash the grease out of your hair."

"That is the idea with your hair, but Kayla's got some Randy in her and his part needs some grease."

Karen smiled, knowing full well she had no idea what I was talking about.

"We'll go the beauty-supply store after we eat."

After lunch we decided to walk to the courthouse, where I was supposed to get some paperwork I needed to take with me to the SBA office. I knew it was the spot when I first saw it. Karen had just switched Kayla to the other hip for the third or fourth time when I saw that sign: FOR RENT 888-249-0568. It was a storefront that looked like the perfect size and location for my shop. I ran toward the sign and poked my head against the dirty glass window just inches from the sign. I grabbed my cell phone before I had time to talk myself out of it.

Within seconds Karen and Kayla were peering into the empty dirt trap with questioning expressions. Even Kayla looked like she thought I was crazy. I guess she was wondering why Auntie Jess got so excited about an empty store. When she pressed her little face against the glass, she probably expected to see something, anything except the wooden slats and half broken-down shelving that had obviously been left behind by the last business that was there.

"Yes, I'm there now. Are you in the area? I'd like to see it as soon as possible."

The man who identified himself as Edgar Williams was on his way down to show me the store. I don't know what I was thinking. I hadn't gotten my financing yet. What would I tell Mr. Williams when he showed up wanting to know if I could afford the place? I stood with my face against that glass until I had fogged it up and couldn't see through. Kayla thought it was a fun game, so she started doing her own share of fogging. Karen held on to her hand as she dragged her back and forth trying to fog as much space as possible, and then going back over it once the remnants of her hot breath disappeared.

Mr. Williams arrived just as he said he would and unlocked the door to what would soon become my shoe and handbag shop. The space was 60x80 with a stairway in the middle of the store that led to a loft area that provided another 12x14. I took Mr. Williams's card and agreed to call him as soon as I got word from the bank.

Karen, Kayla, and I stopped at Barbara's Beauty World just down the street from the vacant building. I picked up Baby Love shampoo, conditioner, and moisturizer. I grabbed five packs of hair bows and a comb and brush that would handle kinky black hair. Karen watched without saying a word or asking any questions. I paid the short Korean sales clerk and nodded to her since she kept nodding at me. Karen still kept silent and juggled a wiggly Kayla from arm to arm.

"What?" Kayla questioned, pointing to the hair care products.

"Things to do your hair with," Karen answered.

Kayla was satisfied with the answer, and it was a good thing since Karen didn't really know what Aunt Jess was buying either.

"Jess, what's wrong with the hair bows I have already?"

"Your baby has a tiny afro right now, those hair bows won't come close to holding that stuff down. Trust me."

We left Barbara's with a white plastic bag full of black hair-care products, and made our way back to Queen's Harbor to teach Karen lesson number one in caring for her daughter's hair.

When we got to the house, I washed Kayla's hair to get the mousse out and then parted each section and spread a little of the hair conditioner on her scalp. Karen was standing over me watching my every move. I think she was making Kayla nervous.

"Cold," Kayla shivered.

"I know honey, but it'll make you look pretty like these girls on the bottle," I said, showing her the picture on the Baby Love bottle.

She smiled and sat still as if she was looking forward to the new look. Karen left the kitchen and came back in a matter of seconds with a notepad and pen.

"What's that for?"

"I'll never remember all this. Got to write it down. So, do I do this every day?"

"Lord hamercy," I sighed.

When I got ready to leave Karen's house, Kayla was playing with Legos and tossing her ponytails from side to side. She loved the new hair. She actually called it new hair. I made sure Karen's notes were complete with daily maintenance instructions and the how-to's for washing and moisturizing the hair.

I left Karen's house with business ownership on my mind. As I drove out the front gate, I could see all the shoes, and a section for handbags. The loft area would be perfect for light hors d'oeuvres and beverages. I wanted the shop to be more than just a place to buy shoes, but rather an experience. I wanted to develop a clientele that did all their shopping with me because of the selection and the service. Since all the shoes and bags I planned to carry were top dollar, I wanted my shop to represent the atmosphere that people with big bucks like.

I stopped at the reception area at the front gate of Queen's Harbor. Just out of curiosity, I walked in to check out the scenery. In all the years Karen and Randy lived there, I had never stopped at the reception area. It was just as I had imagined. The furniture was Ethan Allen and the décor was elegant and stylish. Sure enough, right beside the table used for registration of club activities there were refreshments. Fresh pastries and fruit sur-

rounded an array of beverages from coffee and water to lemonade and soft drinks.

"May I help you with something, ma'am?" the receptionist
asked, stepping in front of her desk.

"No, I'm just looking," I said, as if I were browsing in a department store.

She smiled and nodded her head. This was just the look I was
going for. As I was about to leave, two men walked through the
door to register for the tennis courts. One man signed the paperwork while the other grabbed a couple of bottled waters and
tossed a piece of honeydew in his mouth. He glanced at me,
smiled, and turned around to join his friend. When the two men
walked out, I asked the receptionist why they set the refreshments
out. She cleverly informed me that it was part of the image of the
country club. Queen's Harbor represents the best of everything. No, the refreshments weren't necessary, but why not?
Why wouldn't these patrons think they should have everything?
Exclusivity is the key.

"Find everything okay?" she asked, as I walked toward the
door.

"Got exactly what I needed," I answered, with my heart full
of vision and anticipation.

28

By Christmas, less than five months after my marriage ended, I had completed the training program to start my own business, secured sufficient start-up capital from friends, and found the perfect spot downtown. The only thing standing in my way was the bank making the loan for the rest of what I needed to make sure I didn't end up like many of the small business ventures that sprang up every year. I had been so careful not to mention anything at work or leave any paperwork lying around. The last thing I needed was to lose my only source of income and the avenue for the credential that would hopefully make my résumé shine in that loan office.

On the day that I was supposed to get word of the loan, I paced around the office until I could take it no more. I wrapped up my assignment early and went straight home. Mama was busy in the kitchen preparing one of the boys' favorite meals. Things had taken on a more cordial tone between us, although we still hadn't addressed our issues. I kept busy moving on with my life, and she kept busy tending to the boys, and it kept both of us out of each other's space. I made it clear that my plan was to get the boys and myself out of her place as soon as I got the business off the ground. And that plan hadn't changed, even though I noticed that she was becoming more and more agreeable with each passing day. I didn't dwell on it. The peace was good for the boys, and besides, I had enough to think about with starting my own thing. I trivialized the thought of moving out of Mama's house to the fact that we would no longer get home-cooked meals every day. Mama had raised the bar on dinner preparation and I, for one, was not likely to hit the mark, so that became the subject of most of our conversations.

"You really don't have to cook like this every day, Mama. You gonna spoil my boys," I offered, taking only a small portion of the baked spaghetti.

"Growing boys need to eat. And I see you're starting to fall off yourself. You worried about something?" she asked, and this time it didn't sound like empty conversation, but more like genuine concern.

"Well, now that you mention it. Bank loan," I said between bites.

"What loan? I thought you got money from your friends?"

"I did, but it takes a lot of money to take on a venture like this, Mama. The people at the bank are gonna call today. Soon as I hear something, I can rent the store downtown. The man agreed to hold it until after Christmas, but not much longer," I added, lifting a hefty portion of tossed salad from the bowl. "Things pop up that you didn't expect. And I want my store to be top of the line," I said, still partially waiting for her to bash my dreams.

It was a routine I had grown accustomed to over the years, even though she had been treating me better since the separation.

She walked out of the room, not responding to anything I'd said. I took it as another one of those things she didn't understand or appreciate about me. Just like my decision to join Regina's gym. She talked about how much of a waste it was to pay someone to torture your body like that. I was well on my way to cleaning my plate when she walked back in and reached her hand toward mine.

"Even if the bank does come through, can't hurt to have a little extra, right?" she said, placing a piece of paper in front of me.

I dropped my fork and looked at her with my head tilted to

one side, like she was some kind of foreign creature. I took the paper from her hands. It was a check. I had to look over the amount three times before opening my mouth.

"Mama, I can't take this. You're on a fixed income."

"I know what kind of income I'm on. And why do you have to be so hardheaded?" she interjected, and spun around, walking away from me.

"I really should be fine, Mama. Thanks for the thought," I said, and I meant it.

I felt like she was not only trying to help with the business, but help bridge the gap that had grown in our relationship for years. But I wasn't sure that taking her money was going to help our relationship. All I could think about is that she'd start tossing in her two cents' worth since she had made an investment. I didn't need her control. I didn't want her two cents. So I couldn't take her money.

"Really, Mama, there's no reason the loan shouldn't come through and I'll be just fine," I said, with indignation ringing in my voice.

I was not only turning down her generosity, but further shutting her out of my life. And with the look she turned and gave me, I knew she heard the real sting behind my words.

"Jessi, I haven't always done things right. But it's never been because I didn't want what was best for you," she said, clutching the dishrag from the sink.

Before I could step in and diffuse the situation or stop it from rushing toward some kind of emotional outburst, she spoke again.

"Sometimes mothers want so bad for their daughters to make it that they sabotage it. I started doing that with you, and after a while, I just didn't know how to stop. I was hard because I knew life would be hard, and I wanted you to be strong enough to take it."

"But Mama, in the process you were killing me. Life is hard, but a person needs a place to run for safety. You were never my safe place. You were just as bad as the hard things I kept running into in life," I said, and had to stop myself before I choked on the knot in my throat.

"But look at you now. Despite me, you're still fighting. You're still holding your head up and going on. And starting your own business. Why can't you just let me say I'm sorry?" she yelled, slashing the dishrag across her face.

"That's all I'm trying to do," she continued, and reached for the check that was still sitting on the table beside my empty dinner plate. "I'm sorry, Jessi, and I'm proud of the woman you've become. And I wish I could have said I helped you get to this point." She paused and stepped back toward the kitchen sink, her eyes locking on a faraway place outside the window. "But I can't say I helped. I can't," she offered, and I fought for the words to tell her that it was okay.

But it wasn't okay. I was hurt, scarred, and many times wasn't sure I'd get through all the criticism she'd tossed my way for more than thirty-three years. I couldn't honestly say anything. So I didn't.

"I didn't help then, but I can now. And I will. Whether you take the money or not, I'm going to help you be who you want to be, Jessi," she said and walked out of the kitchen.

The feeling that swept over me after she was gone was more surreal than the phone call that followed. The bank loan officer let me know that I had been approved. It had taken him less than forty-eight hours to go over my plan and grant me the loan. As soon as I hung up the phone with him, I contacted the company renting the space I wanted, rushed out to fill out the application, and officially rented the space. I was glad for the activity. It helped me process what had happened between my mother and me over a dish of spaghetti. Instead of saving some of the errands for another day, I rushed around and completed all of it. I applied for the licenses and filled out more paperwork than I ever thought I would have to just to sell shoes and handbags. And all this just in time for Christmas.

The holidays came and went and I never found a way to bring up the conversation about the check with Mama. I wondered where the money came from. I wondered a lot of things, like what clicked in her brain to make her go from ripping and tearing at my ego to boosting it. What changed her from adversary to investor? But every time I ventured near the topic, she changed the subject.

She, on the other hand, was eager and supportive, and even went as far as throwing a congratulations/New Year's party. She and the boys worked for days getting the house ready. They invited my friends and a couple of people from the church that I didn't hate. Karen and Regina spent the whole time walking around on eggshells waiting for the old Mama to surface. But she never did, and no one dared question why.

As the New Year's ball dropped in Times Square, I looked back over the last few months, barely able to believe that so much had happened so fast. While Mama shoved off to bed and the boys slept right in their spots on the floor in front of the television set, I thought back to how miserable I thought I would be during the holidays. Christmas and New Year's without the normal life we had come to know. But so much had changed and I was so wrapped up in keeping up, I hadn't had time to overeat or overspend. I hadn't even purchased my holiday pair of overpriced shoes, but that would change in a matter of days.

The last thing on my list for starting a business was contacting Straybrook Winslow himself. I've always loved his shoes and I wanted more than anything to carry his line in my store. I sent a formal letter and followed up with a phone call that put me in direct contact with Winslow. I had heard through the grapevine that he is very hands-on with the business, even the process of designing the shoes. He requested a meeting with me, and after spending nearly two hours nursing a bland salad and lukewarm soup, I had the vision of Winslow and a contract to distribute his shoes from my store. The meeting was more like a chat with an old pal than a high-powered business meeting with the leader in shoe designs. While lunching with Straybrook, as he insisted I call him, I told him that I was having trouble coming up with a name for my shop.

"Where did you get the idea for starting a shoe and handbag shop?" he asked, as we walked out of the trendy seafood restaurant.

"Well, believe it or not, it came from my friends; we were

clearing all the shoes and handbags out of my closet after my husband and I separated."

"Then that's your name."

"What?" I stopped dead in my tracks, assuming I had missed something.

"Jessi's Closet," he tossed at me brilliantly, as he smiled, got into his limousine, and whisked off to God only knows where.

During the next three months, I was swamped with everything from securing permits to scrubbing cement floors and washing walls. My March 15th move-in date was upon me before I knew it. The opening would have been a lot easier if I had hired someone to do all the cleaning and manual labor. But trying to be the smart entrepreneur, I chose to do a good deal of the small stuff myself.

I hadn't realized it had been so long since I talked to Karen. We had the usual check-up-on-you conversation. You know, the phone call that lasts about a minute and is filled with courtesy answers because you're too busy to really get into any particular issue. So I was shocked and relieved when I picked up the phone at the shop and heard Karen's voice.

"Jessi's Closet, this is Jessi, how may I help you?"

The phones had been installed and most of the hardware was in the store, but we still had another week or two before the grand opening. It didn't matter to me; I still answered the phone as if I were already open and ready to sell shoes.

"Jessi, I found a lump."

"What? Karen, is that you? You found what?"

The conversation was the last thing I expected, but despite all my busyness I had to put everything down. Karen was crying on the other end of the line, and there was nothing I could do. I couldn't put my arm around her or comfort her. She was miles away and facing the thing she'd most feared since her mother died of breast cancer fifteen years ago.

"Who's there with you? have you called Randy?"

"I just found it, while I was in the shower. I checked and rechecked and it's there in my left breast. Oh God, Jess, what am I gonna do?"

Karen knew her breast like the back of her hand. The doctors had told her about her risks since her mother died so young of breast cancer. Since that day, Karen checked her breast religiously twice a month instead of the once that they recommend. She'd always been paranoid. Once when she was engorged with breast milk after Justin was born, she swore she had cancer and was going to die. Her breasts hurt so badly and there were lumps everywhere. Turned out she had an infection called mastitis that women get after they have a baby. I had gotten a similar call when that happened. But this time there was something different in her voice. There was no postpartum infection possibility. She had found something different in her breasts and neither of us would rest until we found out what it was.

I rushed over to her house to pick her up. There were repair people and inspectors coming by the shop that afternoon, but for the life of me I couldn't focus on any of it. En route to Karen's, I managed to call Mama, who agreed to go to the shop to handle the maintenance people. After catching Mama up on everything and lining up someone to pick the boys up from school, I got Karen back on the line. I couldn't be there with her yet, so I kept her talking on the phone. I'm not sure if that was to help her, or calm my nerves.

"Did you call Randy?"

"I don't want to alarm him if it's nothing."

"I know, but he deserves to know. Call him."

She hung up with me, and called Randy while I called her sitter. She didn't need to face bad news alone, or with me. I was a basket case from the time I heard her say lump. Randy was going to meet us at the doctor's office. The sitter was on the way. When I got to the house, I ran inside and found her in the downstairs bathroom.

"Feel it, Jess," she said, as she lifted her arm straight above her head as if she was reaching to touch the ceiling.

I just stood there looking at her. I wasn't freaked out by touching her breast, but by what I might find when I did. I knew that if I felt something, anything, it wasn't good news. Having a family member die of breast cancer takes your chances up several notches in the high-risk category. And Karen knew those statistics better than the medical personnel who worked with the patients every day. I stood there, still hoping she was wrong and I wouldn't feel a thing.

"Touch it, Jess. Tell me I'm not crazy," she begged.

I reached my hand over and ran it along the outer edge of her breast and then around in a circular motion toward the center.

"It's about the size of a pea—you know, the sweet green peas I make for the children. The ones Justin hates," she continued.

I nodded my head, all the while wondering how you feel something as small as a green pea in your breast. All I could picture was Kayla throwing peas to the floor and watching them roll around. At first I didn't feel anything, but then when I ran my hand along the perimeter again, there it was just to the upper right corner of her right breast. The tears started rolling down my cheeks before I could remove my hand. We both sat down on her bathroom floor like we used to do when we were little girls. Crying and rocking back and forth, not sure what to do next. I was crying just like I had felt the lump in my own body.

"We need to go. They're working me in as soon as I get there. Can you drive me?"

Her request forced me to stop the tears and gain enough composure to get us out of the house, into the car, and headed toward Dr. Baptiste's office. Karen sniffled and mumbled to herself all the way there. I wanted to say something to comfort her, but there were no words. I hated myself for not being better at this. Karen had been so supportive for me during all my hard times. Why couldn't I think of at least one intelligent thing to say to help her during her time of need?

29

Less than an hour after she had phoned me at the shop, we were pulling up at Women's Clinic with an emergency appointment to see Dr. Baptiste, Karen's obstetrician. I spotted Randy's truck and then looked at the front entrance, and he was already standing there waiting. Maybe he would have something helpful to say. Somebody needed to do something; I was no help.

I gave Karen and Randy their privacy, went in ahead of them, and let the receptionist know she was on her way in. The waiting room was filled with women of all sizes and shapes. Some with protruding bellies full of nine months of wonder and some with just full bellies. There were old women and young ones and one teenager with her aggravated-looking mother. I wondered what they were waiting for. The pregnant women were obviously waiting for pregnant-woman stuff, but the others—were they getting yearly physical exams, or was there another woman sitting there afraid to hear those dreaded words, "you have cancer?"

Karen and Randy finally came in and took a seat beside me. Karen shifted nervously in her seat and cried openly right there in the waiting room in front of ten to twelve strangers. Some of the ladies looked away, giving her privacy in a very non-private situation. A few others stared straight on, smiling as if the couple had learned of some good news. The teenager rolled her eyes and looked out the window behind her seat.

"Karen St. Clair . . ."

The nurse motioned for Karen to come back behind the double doors. Randy followed. I stood up while they walked through the doors. The doors closed behind them and I sat, not knowing what else to do. Not able to do anything else but pray. That's right, pray you fool, I said to myself.

They were back there for what seemed like hours, but by the time Randy came out, I glanced at my watch and it had only been forty minutes.

"They're doing X-rays and blood work and all kinds of stuff. Doc feels the lump too, but we still have hope that it's nothing," Randy said, his voice cracking between words.

"How is she?"

"A wreck."

"Anything I can do?"

"Yeah, go on and get some rest. She'll need you after we leave here. I never know what to say or do when she's like this. She'll want you."

He had no idea how inadequate I felt. But it was no time to be petty. I nodded my head and agreed to go on home.

"What about the kids?"

"Sitter's gonna stay on, but you can go to the house if you want and wait for us there."

"Okay," I said, grabbing my purse to leave, only wishing I could be back there with her.

"Oh, Jess. Pick up something for her. Something from all of us, you, me, the kids, and Regina. You're good at that. Something to let her know she's not in this by herself."

I nodded and smiled as Randy made his way back through the double doors. Whatever would I get? And no, I'm not good at this kind of stuff. I cried all the way back to the shop. Cleansing tears that had to come out now, so I could be strong for Karen later that evening.

Later that night, we all gathered around the lanai at Randy and Karen's. The sitter had put the kids to bed, so Karen and

Randy were free to assess the situation. She and Randy talked in unison, one picking up when the other lost the composure to continue.

"They say early stages, but it's aggressive . . ."

"It's like that with younger women, more aggressive I mean. He says we have two options, what they call lumpectomy . . ."

"That's where they take out the portion where the cancerous cells are, or take the whole breast." Karen and Randy both paused after that statement.

The room was so quiet we could hear each other's breaths and thoughts.

"We only have a matter of days to decide which and then I have to do chemo and maybe radiation . . ."

"That's if any of the cells got into her lymph nodes," Randy ended the explanation.

The two looked wiped out just from hearing themselves say the hard words. I didn't know what to say. I watched the two of them. Randy got up to throw away some of the wet tissue that was all over the floor. The tears had been flowing too fast to do much more than drench tissue and grab for more.

By ten o'clock Regina arrived, and we sent Randy to bed. The three of us moved from the lanai to the kitchen, where I made hot tea.

"Green tea. That's what I always drink because something in it is supposed to decrease your chances of getting breast cancer," Karen said in a muffled tone.

We sipped green tea and looked around the kitchen as if assessing the meaning of life. Hearing the word cancer does that to you, makes you see the reality of your own mortality. After spending all those years in church with Derrick I had learned a thing or two about prayer, so I grabbed my girl's hands and prayed. Nothing earth-shattering, just our sincere thoughts.

"Amen," they both said when I was done, wiping tears and sipping more green tea.

I handed Karen the little wind chime I had picked up after I left the doctor's office. Karen took the chime, held it out so the seven tiny metal pipes brushed up against each other, making a sound that reminded me of church bells ringing. She read the inscription.

"What Breast Cancer Cannot Do: Cancer is so limited, it cannot cripple love, shatter hope, corrode faith, eat away peace, destroy confidence, kill friendship, shut out memories, silence courage, invade the soul, reduce eternal life, quench the Spirit, or lessen the power of the resurrection."

I sat up most of the night telling Mama what had happened. She listened and offered encouraging words and a few stories of her friends that had beat cancer. After we were done talking about Karen, she took my day planner and let me know that she would handle all of my business-related appointments and take care of getting the boys to and from school. She rushed off to bed and I did the same, although I slept for no more than two hours before my eyes popped open. I called Regina to see where we were going to meet.

Dr. Baptiste was scheduled to see Karen at 8:00 the next morning to talk about the options. Karen and Randy left for the hospital while Regina and I waited at their house for the sitter to arrive. Then we left, going about our day, as if we would be able to do anything productive with our friend's health hanging in the balance. I met Mama at the shop, shuffled papers for no more than an hour, and then concluded that I wasn't getting anything done. Regina didn't bother to fool herself at work. When I drove up to the hospital front gate, I spotted her car. She was sitting there reading a book about breast cancer and testimonies from survivors.

"She can beat this thing. People beat it every day."

"But she's scared because of her mom. Part of beating it is positive attitude. She's so scared; she's already thinking the worst."

I didn't bother to tell Regina that after she had dozed off last night, Karen asked me to take care of the kids for her. When she first brought it up, I couldn't speak. What do you say to someone who fears her own death, but wants you to raise her children? I just nodded, instead of trying to tell her she was going to be all right. I didn't know that for sure. Telling her something like that wouldn't do her any good. For now, she needed to get facts and make decisions: lumpectomy or mastectomy?

Regina grabbed burgers and fries from the hospital soda shop and we ate outside. The sun was bright and warm. After a few bites, the grease was laying heavy on my stomach, so I tossed the rest of my lunch into the trash bin near the sliding door at the front of the hospital. No sooner than I got it into the bin, the doors slid open and Randy stepped out.

"Figured you two were close by. Didn't imagine this close."

We both looked at him, afraid to speak. Afraid to ask the question, not sure we wanted the answer.

"They're gonna take both breasts, Monday morning. We think it's best."

30

During the next couple of months, Karen had one breast removed, another one reconstructed, and started chemo and radiation. It turns out some of the cells had gotten into her lymph nodes. The days were filled with a whirlwind of activity from juggling the kids, to comforting Karen, to just plain twiddling our thumbs not sure what to do next. Karen was open about everything; she even let us see the new breast. It looked more like a shoulder stuck on the side of her chest. A mound of nippleless pink flesh. She said they were going to add the nipple later. I didn't bother to ask what that was all about. Somehow, thinking about how they'd reconstruct a nipple was beyond my realm of imagination.

When Karen started chemo, the American Cancer Society set her up with a local wigmaker who designed a piece to look just like Karen's natural hair. The day Karen picked up her new hair, she called Regina and me and invited us over for the head-shaving party. I wasn't about to refuse, although I didn't know how I'd sit there and watch my best friend go through this life-changing ritual. She even suggested I bring the boys and Mama. And to my surprise, they all wanted to come. Mama and I sat the boys down and explained what breast cancer was and what Aunty Karen had gone through. They listened and asked intelligent questions. By the time we were done, they couldn't wait to go to the head-shaving party.

Randy had bought wine for us and grape juice in a pretty wine-like bottle for Karen and the kids. There were cheese and crackers sitting out on a tray when we walked in. The room was scented with cinnamon and apple candles and Karen was dressed in a sexy black number that to my surprise was low-cut.

"Looking pretty good, don't you think?" Randy said, grasping the new breast in his hand and giving Karen a seductive wink.

Regina stormed in and paused only long enough to make a crude comment about Randy groping Karen. We sat down to wine and cheese as Randy set up the tall bar stool in the kitchen and plugged in the clippers. We gathered around Karen, who hadn't stopped smiling. Randy started with mushy talk about how much he loved Karen and this experience had only made him appreciate her more. She smiled, sipped more grape juice, and then the buzz started. Randy ran the clippers over the top of her head, right down the middle, Mohawk style. The soft blonde pieces fell to the kitchen floor along with my tears. He handed the contraption to me and I did likewise. After I cut my streak, I gave Karen a tight hug and handed the clippers to Regina. We went all around the room, even Josh, Jared, and Mama. By the time the ceremony was done, Karen was bald and covered in hair and tears. Randy held out the mirror as she placed the wig on her head, a hairpiece they called "Perfect Friend." Strange yet appropriate name for a wig, I thought, as we just watched, speechless.

Breast cancer and all the things that come with it are not the kind of things any of us wants to face, but I was assured that if I had to go through it, this would be the best way to do it. Surrounded by love and openness. Nothing hidden, no pity parties, everything a celebration of the things we were thankful for.

Going through so much with Karen actually helped my relationship with my mother. For so many years we had fought against each other. A secret war going on in our hearts and heads. A war that started when my dad left us nearly twenty years ago. In Mama's earnest efforts to protect me, she simply made me a war casualty. Her explanation was the answer I had all but given up on ever getting. Even after the day she gave me the very large sum of money to help start my business.

"I ran him away," she said, after I had spent two hours crying about Karen's turmoil.

"Who, Mama?"

"Your daddy. Nagged him to death. He started drinking first. But then I nagged harder. And after a while he just wouldn't listen. He was gone long before he ever walked out the door," she said softly, so soft I had to hold my breath to hear the words.

"And I knew what I had done, but for the life of me, I didn't know how to stop. It's like I was so afraid of losing him I ran him off. Makes no sense," she said, speaking into the air, as if I was not in the room. "And that's the one thing I didn't want for you. So I made it my point to help you." She laughed, but I kept still, her words still soft and difficult to hear.

"When you met Derrick and he was into the church, I just knew you had a good one. And I was gonna help you keep him," she said, looking at me for the first time since she started talking.

"That's not a bad thing, Mama," I returned, feeling the sting of her pain.

"But I was doing the same thing to you that I did to your father. Sometimes you can love people too tight, gotta loosen the grip. Let them be who they are. See what they're made of. Look at you now. You really got something with this shop of yours," she said, and I felt like I grew an inch sitting right there in her living room chair.

I felt like I was up to the challenge of running a successful business, and raising two boys into fine young men. After a few minutes of silence, Mama shuffled off to bed, and I soon followed. I will always remember that night because it was the turnaround point in Karen's recovery. But it was also the night that the war ended and two battle-scarred women laid their cards on the table, calling a truce once and for all.

31

To help deal with the stress of seeing Karen go through chemo, I added a few more activities to my schedule. May was the perfect time to take my workout outside, which gave me the perfect opportunity get off the beaten path a little with my gym activities. They now included yoga and a karate class that had just been added. That class is where I met Todd Williams, my first experience with dating in almost eleven years. Todd started flirting with me the first day I stepped into the class. I wasn't sure why, since I was clearly not the youngest or most attractive female in the bunch.

"Mrs. Andrews, it is Mrs., right?" he asked that first day, trying to get into my business. He was too handsome, too cut, and way too young.

"It's actually Ms. Andrews, and you're right to use Ms. since I am obviously your senior."

He smiled as if I had just given him two nuggets of information he was waiting to hear. Todd always picked me as his partner to demonstrate moves to the rest of the class. He said it was because I caught on so quickly and the other ladies seemed to respect me. I say it was because he wanted any excuse to touch my butt and thighs.

When he asked me out the first time, I thought he was awful

slick. He claimed to be new in town and wanted me to show him around. Little did I know it was his way of spending as much time with me as possible and trying to get to me. It worked. We started Friday night with a trip to St. Augustine. We got there early enough to go to the Mussalem Galleries. Art, oriental rugs, and antiques line every bit of space inside the museum. When Todd suggested it, he acted as if we had just stumbled on the place. He wanted me to think he was cultured and into fine things like oriental rugs and art. I knew better than to think his twenty-five-year-old behind was interested in anything but getting some time in with an experienced woman. As much as I was trying not to be impressed, we had a lot of fun, and even in a museum he had the sense of humor that helped him bulldoze his way into my world.

After the museum we got dinner at Cortess Bistro and Flamingo Room. I had only been there once, but I knew Todd was pulling out all stops to let me know he appreciated the finer things in life. He shelled out a pretty penny on dinner, wine, dessert, and more wine. We walked along the historic streets of St. Augustine, talking and trying to get our heads together for the drive back. A couple of bottles of wine will do a number on you if you aren't careful.

When Todd dropped me off, he quickly threw in his request to see more of the area on Saturday. He had planned some exciting things in Ponte Vedra, so I didn't argue. I needed the break from the shop, and I had promised Karen I would get out and have some fun. He was nice, fun, and the best-looking thing I had seen in some time, so I figured I had nothing to lose. I spent most of Friday night trying not to think about how much fun I'd had with him. But my guard was up. After living so many years with Derrick, trust was not something I was going to do very quickly. And besides, Todd was too young for anything more than a little rebound fling.

Saturday morning came before I knew it. Todd had made reservations at Ponte Vedra Inn and Club's spa. We started with full-body massages, and went on to the hot-paraffin manicure and pedicure and facial. I got my hair and makeup done and

Todd let them cut his hair. I was surprised there was someone who could cut a black man's hair. I guess they'll do anything as long as your money is green and making its way from your hand to theirs. We had lunch right there at the spa and then set out for the beach. I wasn't crazy about going to the beach after getting my hair done and looking and smelling so good. But I enjoyed it. We walked along kicking up sand and cracking jokes about the people at the spa. This young boy was getting to me and I had to admit I could get used to hanging out with him. But I wondered how long he'd be able to keep up his expensive, open-court dating.

After spending an entire weekend with Todd, I decided to keep my distance for a while. He called me every other night and I always came up with an excuse. I really was busy at the shop, but my main reason for holding him off was simply a power move. He had called me three days straight and I didn't want him getting the idea that he was anything more than just a nice guy I enjoyed hanging out with. Although I was physically attracted to him, I didn't want him getting any ideas.

After a week went by, he asked me out for drinks. It seemed harmless enough, but since I wasn't into playing games I let him know early on that I was separated and not ready to get involved with anyone. He didn't seem to mind, just as I thought he wouldn't. A few drinks and pleasant conversation led to dinner a week later, and dinner and movie the next week.

After six or seven dates, Regina and Karen were encouraging me to at least kiss him. I thought it sounded juvenile to sit back with two grown women and talk about a first kiss, but they were so into it. They wanted to know if he looked like he could kiss. I forgot to ask them how a man looks if he is a good kisser. I didn't know there was a way to tell. Regina assured me there's a definite way to tell. Then they got into the size-of-feet conversation, and if I hadn't known better I would have sworn we were right back in high school talking about sex for the first time.

It had been two months since I met him and at least ten dates later before I let him kiss me and talk about going to his place for drinks. He had been the perfect gentleman all along, not pressuring me about the kiss or anything physical. So I agreed to it. We had dinner, went to a movie, and then back to his place for drinks.

His apartment was plainly decorated, exactly like I would expect from a man who had just moved to town and spent several weeks courting me. After the drinks I yawned to signal I was about to leave, but Todd wasn't ready to call it an evening. He begged me to stay a little longer, and I have to admit it was nice to have a man beg to keep me around. After everything I had been through, it was just good to have a man pay attention at all. The diet the girls had put me on was working and I had lost enough weight to have to make some severe changes to my wardrobe. Not enough to go out and get all new clothes, but I had to pull out the old sewing machine and take some of my dresses in a little so they'd fit nicely. That was a good feeling. Todd begging me to stay was another good feeling.

We talked and sipped wine until my head was swimming and my walk was unsteady when I tried to make my way to the door. I knew I shouldn't drive in that condition, but there was no way I was going to stay in this man's house past midnight. When I reached the door and went to grab my coat, Todd grabbed me and pulled me close. He was already breathing in a shallow low tone that told me he was a few steps ahead of me. My mind kicked into high gear, telling me all the reasons to put the brakes on in a hurry. Before I could listen to my heart or head, my body spoke up. Our lips met and parted as we both tried to eat each other up. He acted as starved as I was. He pushed me away slightly, unbuttoned my blouse and fondled my breast as I stumbled backward to his sofa. I leaned back on the top edge of the sofa, opened my legs as he stepped in close enough to let me know exactly how much he wanted me. I don't know what he did first, unbutton his pants or unfasten my bra, but before I knew it, he was nibbling my breast and grinding hard against the ache that was begging him to come on in. We kissed and touched and undressed frantically. We moved from the back edge of the couch to the front where Todd laid down and slid his pants and underwear down. I didn't bother to take my skirt off as I watched him slide the condom on. And then I took over. He let out a deep moan as I eased down on top of him taking in every inch, rocking back and forth. My mind jumped back into the game, trying to figure out what the hell my body was doing. This wasn't my style, no real relationship, no background check to make sure he was who he said he was.

I jumped up, leaving him fully erect and mad as hell.

"What's wrong? What are you doing?"

"I can't do this, not like this. This isn't what I do."

"Wha'cha mean this isn't what you do? You were doing just fine."

"I don't just do this, not like this. I just met you and I'm still married, getting a divorce, but right now . . . I, I just don't do this kind of thing," I mumbled as I dressed and grabbed my handbag and keys.

By now Todd was pulling his pants back on and trying to settle himself down enough to figure out what I was talking about. I couldn't explain myself, and even if I could he wouldn't hear me. All the blood had rushed from his brain to his penis, and that was the only thing he cared about satisfying. I said good night and got out before he had a chance to ask me anything else I couldn't answer. As I ran from his apartment, I couldn't help but wonder which was worse, marriage or dating. With no time to figure it out, I resolved that I wasn't very good at either.

32

I dropped the karate class and changed gyms. I never ran into Todd again after that night. I never mentioned it to Karen since she was a little too prim and proper to imagine such indiscretion. Regina, on the other hand, had plenty to say.

"Girl, ain't nothing wrong wit' getting you some. You need something to help relieve the stress of starting that shop. I saw that karate guy, ain't half bad. Kind of skinny to me, but not bad for a one-night stand."

"Speaking of getting some, I haven't seen much of Reginald lately. Did he fall in?"

She laughed at my sexual humor, but the expression left over after the smile faded said something else was going on with Ms. Regina.

"Okay, what happened? You found out he was married, or had five kids by five different women, or was it jail time?"

"Actually he asked me to marry him. Gave me a ring and everything."

"And that did it for you. Good man plus ring and proposal equals trouble to you, right?"

"I almost considered it. And that's what scared me the most. I haven't seen him in months. I heard he had moved on with some chick he dated back in the day. And I've moved on, too."

All our lives Regina had been moving on, so this latest announcement didn't get a rise out of me. In fact, I had all but
tuned her out until she dropped the bomb.

"In fact, I switched teams altogether. I been seeing someone
I met through work. She's cool; I think you'd like her."

"Her, oh boy. When did you?"

I didn't even know how to ask the question. I had never
known a lesbian up close and personal, and in my mind Regina
just didn't fit my narrow-minded opinion of a woman who dates
women. She was always a diva and had more male skeletons in
her closet than the county graveyard. So how did one go from
hoochie to lesbian overnight?

"You think I'm bullshitting, don't you?"

"You aren't, are you?" I asked, suddenly remembering the
night in the sauna on our Alaska vacation.

She was nodding her head and so was I. Regina had mentioned something about considering women, and with my life
in such turmoil I hadn't given her words a second thought.

"So you were really thinking about this back when we were
in Alaska." I finally got the words to come out.

"You're as smart as I always knew you were. I was just feeling you guys out. To see how you would take it. And I must say,
I didn't get a great response."

"Well, it's a sudden change. Maybe you're just reacting to
the breakup, or maybe what happened with your mom is getting
to you."

"You're probably right. So, I'm dysfunctional. What next,
Dr. Phil?"

I wasn't expecting her to flip the script on me, so I didn't
know how to respond other than watch and wait. Regina had
done irrational things in the past. I assured myself that this was
probably one of those things and she'd get over it. Crazy world.
While I was out acting like a horny teenager, Regina was doing
whatever women do to each other. I wondered, but I wasn't
about to ask. Regina isn't the kind you ask questions like that
unless you want clear, concise, visual details. I let it go, won-

dering how she'd break this wonderful news to prim and proper Karen.

"What else going on with you?" she asked, as the lesbian talk came to an abrupt halt.

"Nothing nearly as interesting as you. Ever."

"Seen that fool lately?"

"He conveniently picks the boys up when I'm not at home and drops them off in like manner. The house has been on the market for some time, but not a nibble yet. I hope something happens by the time the divorce is final."

"How much longer?"

"Too much. Seriously, just another couple of months, but since the boys are out of school for summer, he's supposed to be keeping them until they go back in August."

"Wonder where he's gonna keep 'em. Minnie kicked him out," she said, as casually as she had told me that she was now a lesbian.

And when the conversation was over, I wasn't sure which statement to stay up all night stressing about.

Summer vacation ended with a bang. Derrick was scheduled to drop the boys off the same day that we were supposed to sign the divorce papers, and the papers for the sale of the house. I couldn't for the life of me figure out why he had scheduled everything for the same day, but with no time to sulk or do bodily harm to the man, I agreed to meet him and the realtor at the house. We could sign all the papers in one swing and he could drop the boys off when I wasn't at home, in his usual fashion.

Having shed nearly twenty five pounds from the stress of running my own business, having a friend with cancer, and working out, the slim red dress was hugging me in all the right places. I looked myself over in the mirror as I prepared to see Derrick for the first time since he tore out of my mother's living room a year ago. So many things had changed, but the biggest change was my attitude. I was strong, confident, and self-assured, all the things I lacked not quite a year earlier. I slid my purse onto my arm and spun around to meet the man who had tried to wreck my life and then use my boys to rub my face in it. As I drove along toward the old house, the anger grew to a hot lava in my belly. I could taste the resentment for the way he treated me. I wanted him to pay, but I was intelligent enough to know that seeking revenge on him would only bring me down to his level.

I drove up to the house only to see Derrick's truck parked out front. I slid from the front seat of my car and sauntered up the sidewalk toward the house that looked smaller at first glance. Nothing about the place looked the same, and as I walked through the front door, nothing felt the same. The hallway was empty, no pictures or plants lining it. And there was a musty, closed-in smell that meant no one else had been in the place for a while either. The realtor had said they came in periodically to freshen things up as they showed the place to people. But I assumed that since they hadn't been showing it to anyone, they also hadn't been freshening it.

As I walked through to the kitchen, I spotted Derrick leaning against the counter. His starched, white, button-down shirt and navy khakis had that right-out-of-the-cleaners look. His eyes traced the line of my body from head to toe and then back up again.

"Damn. What have you been doing?"

"Working hard. Someone has to," I threw back at him as I stepped closer to sign the papers he had spread out on the counter.

"Why such a hurry? The realtor will be here soon. I figured we'd take a minute to catch up. I see you been taking real good care of yourself," he said, licking his lips.

The sight didn't sicken me as much as I thought it would. There was a new feeling that came over me. Control. I liked it, so I went with it.

"Since you're in such a hurry, what do you say we get this wrapped up and grab a bite?" he added, as his eyes dropped down to my behind.

I ignored him and signed the papers. I stacked them neatly in a pile and turned to leave. He reached for me and pulled me back to him, close enough that I could smell his cologne, or some woman's leftover perfume. I wasn't sure which because it smelled sweet and feminine.

"How 'bout a little kiss for old times' sake. You know, no hard feelings."

I couldn't believe he had the audacity to stand right in front of me and ask for physical affection and say that there were no hard feelings. My feelings were very hard, but they had started to betray me. I stepped closer to him, leaned in and kissed him on the cheek.

"No, baby. You can do better than that," he insisted.

So I did. I stepped closer, placed my hands in the middle of his chest, at the opening between buttonholes. In one swift motion I yanked the shirt open, sending tiny buttons all over the clean, vacant kitchen. As the tiny plastic pieces hit the floor, I started kissing his chest soft and tender just at the base of his neck. Slow, random kisses down to his left nipple, and then the right. I heard him swallow hard, as I worked my tongue down his torso to his belly button, where I bit him gently as his starched khakis pressed against my throat, almost cutting off my breath. He let out a shallow moan, as I made my way back up to his neck, then his ear taking the entire lobe into my mouth. He reached for me, and I slapped his hands down.

"Not in a million years," I whispered, grabbing my purse and walking toward the front door.

He was mumbling something as he reached for me. The realtor was walking through the front door as I walked out. She paused briefly, taking in Derrick's bare chest and ripped-open shirt. Not to mention his heavy breathing.

"Is this a bad time?" she asked, apologetically.

"Not at all. Just selling a house, and getting a divorce. The papers are inside. Thank you for your time," I said, and walked down the driveway to my car, and took my rightful place in the driver's seat.

33

The summer ended, the kids went back to school, and hurricane season kicked off. The final divorce papers came in the mail, along with a check for my portion of the house sale. Without a second thought, I filed the papers, deposited the check, and went on with my day. The papers were only the official notification of something that had happened long ago. Derrick and I had divvied everything else we owned, and other than two wonderful boys there was no sign of the fact that we had ever been together.

In September, instead of whisking off to Alaska, I decided it was time to take Jessi's Closet to the next level. And just like clockwork, the next phase seemed to drop into my lap.

One of Regina's male conquests, before she started dating women, happened to play golf and met some of the folks who organized the annual Player's Championship in TPC Sawgrass Stadium. Well, one conversation led to another, and somehow my name and shop got mentioned in one of them. When the PGA guy called me about the contract, I thought it was someone playing a practical joke. I agreed to meet with him over lunch to discuss the details. They were looking for another sponsor for the event as well as for a number of small tournaments throughout the year. Their efforts to reach into the African

American community and bring in African American–owned businesses had failed—until he found me. It was the perfect marriage proposal. I agreed to be a cosponsor for the golf events if they sent paying customers my way. They even let me set up shop at the stadium during the tournament, to get the stragglers looking for the latest shoes the pros were wearing.

Of course, no sooner than my lunch digested, I was on the phone with a representative at Winslow to set up a separate account dealing with golf shoes. A little online research led me to a company in San Ramon, Spain, willing to supply shoes and handbags for women and golf handbags for men. That's right. There's a handbag that men carry when playing golf. I had no idea. It's a handbag all right, but it's okay because it's for golf and it's expensive and masculine looking. All the high-rolling, chic golfers carry them, so I put in my order for a buttload of them.

My little shoe-and-handbag shop had gone from a hopeful idea born out of my own obsession to a virtual empire of shoes and handbags for just about every occasion. Just hours after getting the contract, and ordering the supply of golf shoes and bags, I had rented a space in Ponte Vedra and officially named it Jessi's Hole In One. That shop would be the golf center, equipped with staff knowledgeable of the game and ready to help tournament players get the latest to hit the greens. I found out what golfers like to munch on while they putter around shopping, so the back bar area of Hole In One would be stocked with trays of finger sandwiches to eat and hot and cold beverages. Jessi's Closet and Jessi's Hole In One would represent the most unique shoe-buying concept in the area.

Most folks would look at my actions and think I was just a little over the top. The ink was not even dry on the contract and there I was renting shop space and buying stuff. Well, there was one thing I learned all those years of working for someone else: The prize goes to the one who gets there first. If this thing didn't take off, it would not be because I'd dragged my feet and been slack. I was on top of the moment and ready to meet the challenge head-on. While I was out renting space and making orders, someone at the Small Business Administration got word of my accomplishment and spent the next six months keeping a close eye on Jessi Andrews, female entrepreneur.

By spring, my success was all that anyone in the city could talk about. My mind, however, was on weightier matters. Regina had still not told Karen that she was gay. Josh and Jared were both playing every sport the school would allow, which kept me running from one end of the city to the other for games. Mama was sulking because the boys and I had moved into our own place. And I hadn't had a date since the awful mishap with Todd the karate instructor nearly a year ago.

Being the most successful new business owner in Jacksonville didn't afford me the opportunity to grovel, so I got up each morning at 4:00 a.m. for exercise and prayer, and then spent the next ten to twelve hours saving the world. Or at least keeping them in sensible shoes. And to make it all worth the trouble, the Small Business Administration was preparing to honor me at the yearly banquet. Somehow one of the big boys found out about my negotiations with the PGA people, and one thing led to another. Suddenly middle-aged white men by the dozens were calling to schedule appointments with me to talk about profit margins and leveraged buyouts. Life was going great, and as if the news couldn't get any greater, the boys announced that they couldn't spend the upcoming weekend with their dad because his girlfriend had kicked him out. I fought the urge to call and invite him to the banquet. As Mama would say, "That's just plain ugly, Jessi."

34

May 20th, 2005

Mr. Ty Basnight finally returns with the paperwork and a smile. Thinking back over the past year and a half while Ty is out of the office, gives me a new sense of perspective. It also gives me a feeling of boldness. I ask him to join me at the banquet. He seems harmless enough, and besides, couldn't hurt to have a banker in my pocket. Also couldn't hurt to have him somewhere else too, but that would come later.

I walk out of the bank feeling pretty good about everything except the nagging uneasiness in my stomach. The steady beeping coming from my brown leather handbag startles me as I shift my stride to the less busy area of the sidewalk, hit the send button, and continue my pace.

"Hello, this is Jessi."

"Jessi, how did it go, or do I even need to ask?" an eager voice chants in my ear.

"Karen, you would not believe how much they offered me for the line. Girl, I'll just say, lunch is on me," I giggle, ducking in and out of dark suits without faces.

"Oooo, we need to celebrate. What time is Regina getting to town?"

"What time is she supposed to get here, or what time will her slack behind actually show up?" I say, as Karen gives distracted instruction in her sternest mother tone to Kayla.

"Okay, Jess, well, pick me up after you're done at the bank. The sitter canceled, but Randy had a light day, so he's coming home to watch the kids. Kayla just pooped in the potty, so I've got to run."

She hangs up before I can say goodbye, but that's well enough since I need to cross the street to get to the parking garage. The cars along Main Street come to a screeching halt as I watch the little orange man at the top of the post signaling me to walk, all the while thinking of the prospect of wiping a child's poopy behind. Glad those days are long gone.

I get into my car and start the long drive from downtown to Queen's Harbor. The thought crosses my mind that it might have been a mistake to invite a total stranger on a date. But I had this crazy feeling before I gave him the invitation. It has to be something else. Perhaps lunch with the girls will reveal the cause. Or something terrible will happen at the banquet. I'll be on my way up to the podium to accept an award, step on the front of my dress, trip and fall facedown into the lap of the PGA representative. Whatever it is, I know what it can't be: finding my husband with another woman. Been there, done that.

I almost miss the turn to Karen's neighborhood as the tears form in my eyes simply from thinking about how much has happened since that awful day. As I approach the front gate at Queen's Harbor, the short, tight-faced lady walks out to the car. I assume she is ex-military since her back never bends, her head stays straight forward, and her expression is something between pissed-off and uncertain. She has everything except the navy uniform. As soon as she sees my face, she waves and turns back around. Queen's Harbor is a gated community: no entrance unless you have permission or a damn good way with words. I pass the rows of overpriced pink, beige, and pale green stucco homes located right off the golf course. I always wondered how many times the owners had to replace windows knocked out by wayward golf balls. There are three men standing around a green looking down at the tiny white ball and then at the flag stick marked fourteen. Two years ago the sight of men who owned homes like these, playing golf in the middle of the day, ticked me off. Today I tilt my head in their direction, knowing thousands of those recreational dollars are now coming my way.

"Play on golfers, play on . . ." I yell, mocking Jay Anthony Brown of the *Tom Joyner Morning Show*.

The homes toward the front of the neighborhood are for the avid golfers; the homes toward the back for the boaters. Karen and Randy do neither, so their home is one of the less expensive ones with just grass and trees, no lake or golf course. In my earlier years as a married, mid-range, single-family homeowner, I always thought these places were excessive. People with too much money and not enough compassion. I always thought if I had that kind of money, I'd do something productive and helpful with it. Then again, we say a lot of things when we're spending money that isn't our own.

The yardman is trimming hedges when I drive up to Karen's house. Her truck is sitting in the driveway, clean as a whistle with water still beading on the exterior. Just as I turn the engine off, another man walks from behind the house with a towel and starts wiping the truck. I get out of my own car, ignoring the dirt so thick I could send a message to aircraft flying above.

I walk into the house without knocking. Karen knows I am coming; she is always either changing someone or feeding someone, so I make it easy on her and let myself in. Sure enough, Kayla is sitting in the high chair covered in spaghetti noodles and applesauce. Karen walks around the corner with an equal amount of the food on her navy, button-down, short-sleeve J. Crew.

"Gotta change Jess, make yourself at home. There's lemonade on the lanai, fresh squeezed, see?" she says, pointing to a big round wet stain on her skirt.

I nod my head and watch her dash down the hall toward the laundry room. Kayla is still slinging spaghetti noodles around the kitchen, so I opt for the lanai before I too need a change of clothes. I notice Karen is still wearing the wig even though her hair is coming back in.

With a glass of lemonade in hand I sit down to watch a young, handsome, shirtless man doing yard work in the back of the house. He too is trimming hedges while beads of sweat run down his hairless chest.

"My, my, my," I whisper, and turn my attention to the new plants Karen has set out near the lanai. Not that I want to look at plants, but that boy is too young for me to get another eye-. ful. Despite myself, I glance back at him, thinking he looks kind of familiar. He finishes the bushes near the pool and moves to the ones closer to the lanai, and that's when I realize he *is* familiar. He was the guy with the maxed-out credit card at the hotel the night of Hurricane Lily, the night I found my husband doing nasty at the car dealership. Small world.

Kayla starts screaming and I am grateful for the diversion. I take another quick sip of the lemonade and make my way back into the kitchen. Kayla is done tossing noodles and can't see through all the sauce covering her eyelids. I walk toward the baby girl, not sure what I plan to do. I certainly am not going to touch spaghetti girl and mess up my clothes, too. I am saved by the mom. Karen rushes in from the laundry room with a towel that looks more like a blanket. She swoops Kayla out of the chair and rushes off down the hall—to wherever mothers go with children covered in food—just as the phone rings.

"Get that, Jess . . . hands full."

It's Regina, promising to be at the restaurant on time. I answer politely, knowing full well she hasn't been on time a day in her life.

"Who was it?"

"Just Regina."

"What'd she want?"

"Nothing, you 'bout ready?"

Karen walks into the kitchen holding a naked, dripping wet Kayla, bursts into tears, and slumps down right there on the floor, wet baby and all.

35

I take the shivering Kayla out of Karen's arms and wrap her in the towel.

"Mommy sad," she says as I hurry her off down the hall to her bedroom to find something to put on her chill-bump-covered body. Children seem to adjust so well to their parents' insanity. Within seconds Kayla's concern for her mom is diverted to trying to pick the tiny beaded things off my blouse.

"Yes, Mommy sad, but she'll be okay. Now tell Aunty Jess where your clothes are, okay?" I say in my most mothering voice, which still feels somehow shy of nurturing and compassion.

I can hear Karen moving around in the kitchen. I want to check on her, but Kayla's hands won't fit through the armhole of the shirt, so I have to yank that one off and find another one. Outside Kayla's window I can see Karen walking through the yard toward a small flower garden near the woods. I wrestle with Kayla, trying desperately to get something onto her naked body before she shakes herself into a frenzy. Karen sits on a bench beside the garden, staring off into the distance. I figure she needs space, so I make my peace to do something close to dressing her child in clothes that won't cut off her circulation. I finally come across a Barney shirt that looks too big. Perfect, I think, as I yank it down over Kayla's tiny torso.

When Karen finally walks back to the house and sits down on the lanai, I am embarrassed by my selfishness. Thinking about my own screwed-up life, when my best friend just slumped down weeping in the fetal position on her kitchen floor. I have Kayla dressed, hair pulled back into something close to a ponytail and sitting quietly in front of the TV set watching four grown white men jumping and singing like spastic children. Justin, Karen's four-year-old, finally makes an appearance.

"Hi Aunt Jess, Daddy here yet?" he says, before joining Kayla on the floor. I shake my head and watch as both kids sit clinging to every word of the song about riding in a big red car. I glance at my watch and it is close to 11:00—time to go, if we are going to avoid the heaviest part of the downtown traffic. I walk to the lanai where Karen is sitting, sipping lemonade.

"I'm pregnant Jess, shhhh, the kids don't know."

We hug and I cry right along with her. I don't want her to feel strange for collapsing in the middle of the floor with her naked baby in her arms. I stand back and pat her belly, still flat as it ever was. Part of me envious of her life. Part of me loving the freedom of being able to follow my dreams on my own terms, but still part wanting to learn how to fix a little girl's hair, and laugh and play while watching the men who call themselves "Wiggles," whatever the hell that means.

Karen goes to touch up her makeup and clean herself up for the third time today. I watch Kayla and Justin and the wiggly men, trying desperately not to envy. I have no right to envy Karen. My life hasn't been wonderful every day, but the good outweighs the bad. I think of Karen, Randy, and the kids: the perfect couple in their immaculate home. Rich, successful, and favorites around Queen's Harbor.

"Hey girl, where's your mind?" Randy says, walking up and grabbing me like he hasn't just seen me two days ago.

"Waiting for your wife. How many times does she dress each day?"

He looks around the kitchen for signs of the mess that has caused yet another wardrobe change. I have cleaned most of it, but notice a few strings of spaghetti still clinging to the legs of the high chair.

"Kayla, huh . . . yeah, that's how it is when they start trying to feed themselves. More food on the floor and wall than inside the kid."

"Oh, congratulations. Sounds like you got some swimmers, man."

"Ahhh, you know. No need to brag, but you know I put it down," he says, beating his chest like an ape with too much ego.

"Where you guys going today? Please tell me you aren't planning another one of those girl trips. What made you fools go to Alaska anyway?"

I shrug my shoulders like a woman with a secret as Randy goes upstairs to check on Karen. The most bizarre vacation three women could ever take, I think, as Kayla and Justin put on another tape of those Wiggling men.

In no time Karen comes bounding down the stairs shouting orders back at Randy. "And don't forget to give Justin his allergy medicine before he takes his nap."

When I look back at the television, the Wiggly men are still jumping about singing with a man in a dog costume that looks like it has seen better days. I listen as Karen barks out orders and Randy nods his head, only half acknowledging her. Kayla douses her with wet kisses as we head out the door. Justin tries to be four-year-old macho, but ends up throwing his arms around Karen's neck and planting a sloppy one on her left cheek.

"She's coming back guys, go on back in and play. See ya baby," Randy says to Karen as he shuts the door and goes to play Mr. Mom.

"We'll take my car," I suggest, not expecting Karen to disagree. She still looks a little shaken from the incident in the kitchen. Must be hormones, I think as I hit the alarm button and wait for the two chirping noises that let me know the doors are unlocked. Wouldn't want to jiggle the door handle before the alarm is disengaged; the sirens going off would put all of Queen's Harbor on alert. No need to force the residents to give us a second look.

They are trying desperately to act like it doesn't bother them to see our black faces going in and out of these near-million-dollar homes. I start the engine and pull out of the driveway, only briefly catching a glimpse of the older black man still making his way around the hedges in the front yard. He has a paternal look with an angelic face that makes his smile and nod feel more like a gesture of approval. As I pull out of the driveway, I notice how at home he seems with the land, like he belongs in the garden. I smile, knowing there is likely always a hefty amount of dirt lodged under his nails, and that's just fine with him.

I watch as Karen waves to the round lady at the front gate. I too throw my hand up. It's the rule. Make good with the front gate people. They can get sudden amnesia if you are rude with them. One of Karen's neighbors spent two hours trying to get home, all because he had pissed off a front-gate guy and then forgotten to update the code on the front and rear of his vehicle.

That's how they know you belong. The gate has a sensor that responds to a bar code along the front and rear of your bumper. The codes have to be updated each year, just to make sure there isn't anyone getting in who shouldn't.

I pass through the second stoplight headed down Atlantic, and there is yet another gated community. Nice houses, gates, security. Who are they trying to keep out—or in, for that matter?

Karen fumbles through her purse, looking for lipstick I assume, since her lips are bare and in need of chapstick or anything. She pulls out a stale cookie and a Lego block before she gets to the lipstick tube. The traffic going into downtown isn't as bad as I thought it would be. Karen has snapped out of her daze and is ready to talk.

"Jess, you really look good. That dress is you. How much have you lost?" Karen says, still rubbing her lips together to spread the lipstick evenly.

"Probably thirty. I'm not really scale-watching right now. I feel good, and I like the way I look, so the amount of weight and all that doesn't matter anymore."

"You weren't too happy when Regina mentioned it in Alaska."

"Damn straight. Who wants their best girlfriends telling them they need to lose weight, fix their hair, and get some better clothes, especially after she just found her husband screwing a Toni Braxton look-alike?"

A blaring horn gets my attention. The light has turned green, but I am still sitting there, thinking about Alaska and the hope that was in my heart as we made the trip back home. It seems like such a long time ago. So much has happened.

"You look good, too. And now pregnant. Must feel good, after everything."

She nods, touching her wig and still rubbing her lips together.

"It's so funny. The receptionist at the place where I got the radiation treatments used to stare at my head from the time I walked in until I left. I was so self-conscious thinking it was lopsided or something. And then one day, she stopped me and asked who does my hair. I paused, just knowing she wasn't making some rude joke. Turns out she thought this was my hair and was jealous because it was always in place and looked so nice," she laughs.

"You're joking me."

"No. Now how stupid can you be? So, I just went along with it and gave her the name of my old hairdresser."

"You didn't!"

"Yep, dumb bitty. I'm gonna wear it until my hair fills in better. It looks okay right?" she asked, adjusting it again.

"Of course it does. If you can just keep Kayla from snatching it off in public," I add, reminding Karen of the pleasant dinner at Enrique's when she suddenly went bald at the hand of her two-year-old.

By the time we get downtown, all of the free and metered parking on the street is taken. Without complaining, I drive around to the parking garage and bite the bullet. Eight dollars to park all day. Four for a half day. With my luck I'll go just past the half-day mark, and have to pay the full eight. Karen's phone rings again. Regina. The thirty-minute drive and ten minutes of parking roulette has gotten the best of me as Karen nods her head in response to late-ass Regina.

"If she'd stop calling so much, she could get here on time," I say as Karen puts her index finger over her tightly clamped lips.

36

"So Hooters it is," Karen says in response to Regina's request. Jacksonville Landing has several nice places to grab a bite at lunch, but Regina wants Hooters, so who are we to argue? Karen and I leave the parking garage to the tune of the one chirp signaling my alarm is set. We cross the street to the landing, lifting an eye to the statue of Andrew Jackson tipping his hat while his horse's front legs kick into the air. Karen is still too quiet for my taste. Her silence is giving me too much time to think.

We pass an espresso shop perched on a tiny cart. A woman in jeans and a faded Van Halen t-shirt is twirling her thumbs around each other as she sits on a bar stool that is moaning under the weight of her substantial rear end. I look her way and nodd. She smiles a near-toothless grin and returns to her distant stare and thumb twirling. Espresso on wheels. I think not.

Ducking in and out of schoolchildren, Karen and I make our way to the restaurant. I look ahead to see why the kids are in such a hurry. The blinking lights at Gator World confirm my suspicions. Video games and junk food.

"Table for two?" the waitress asks.

Karen gives her our seating request while I check out the skimpy, low-cut shirt and shorts that give a hefty peek at two tight and toned butt cheeks. We follow her to a table with three chairs around it. We thank Butt Cheek and take our seats, flipping through the menus and checking out the other patrons at the same time.

"Why you so quiet?"

"A lot on my mind. But this is good. Out with the girls . . . and your big event tonight."

"Nothing really, just some stupid pat-me-on-the-back banquet for all the SBAs in the area. Truth be known, I'd rather head over to Pom's and get some Thai."

"Ladies, ladies, ladies . . . whazzzup?" Regina almost yells, drawing attention from everyone in the restaurant.

Regina has actually toned down her wardrobe a lot lately. She is sporting a pair of yellow cotton shorts with a matching sleeveless jacket to show her bulging biceps. She likes showing her muscles. She says it intimidates men so they know not to give her any shit. Her hair is shoulder-length, hanging straight with just a part down the middle. No jewelry and only white ankle socks and solid white Reeboks on her feet. Even her purse is modest, a tiny black shoulder-sling bag only large enough to hold driver's license, credit card, and a little cash.

"What's happening, Karen . . . oh Jess, how did your thing go?"

"She nailed it, of course. Lots of money and the respect she deserves," Karen chimes in, answering for me.

"And the banquet tonight. Whatcha wearing? Karen, you need to wear something to show off those new titties. You seen the nipples, Jess?"

"No I haven't had the pleasure yet."

"It's nice. A tattoo," Regina adds, like I haven't heard that much.

I don't want to look too shocked and make Karen feel bad. Regina takes over the explanation of the nipple tattoo. She describes the color and everything. Someone told Karen to get a darker color than her real nipple had been because the tattoo fades over time. The whole thing is more than I can fathom, but I still sit there trying to picture what it looks like and what makes it fade over time, and how much Karen's has faded in the last few months.

I scan the restaurant while Karen and Regina go toe to toe on which dress will show the new boobs best. Watching people has become my new pastime. Watching and listening to conversations. All business owners should do it. Lets you know what people are into, what they want. That'll be chapter one in the book I'm gonna write someday about running a successful business. "Stop, look, and listen" is the title.

Butt Cheek walks by, giving Regina one last stab at getting Karen to show up sporting a crop top and a thong. Karen gets her back by dropping the baby bomb on her. I watch as Regina congratulates and Karen cries, again.

It was nothing short of a miracle that Karen didn't have to get a hysterectomy when she was getting her breast removed and going through treatment. She said the doctor assured her the chemo shouldn't have any effect on the baby. After Regina gets all the details of Karen's pregnancy, the attention shifts to Regina's date.

"So, are you bringing someone tonight?" I ask, already knowing the answer.

"Why you got to be an instigator?"

Regina and I go back and forth as I try to pry into her business, but both of us fail to see that Karen isn't taking part in our game. She gets our attention when silent sobs turn to snotty outburst. Karen jumps up from the table and rushes off to the ladies' room. I am right on her heels, hoping it's the pregnant hormones and not another life-changing event like breast cancer.

"I sent a letter to my father," she whispers as Regina and I walk into the stall behind her.

There is barely enough room for one person in that stall, but somehow the three of us manage to squeeze in. There are three or four ladies washing their hands and touching up makeup, so the only privacy we have is the single bathroom stall.

"You did what?"

"I wrote him a letter. I found out where he lives and sent him a letter about what's going on with me now. He knows about Randy and the kids."

"What made you do that? I thought you didn't want to see him ever again."

"After I got cancer, I started thinking about it. And so, I wrote the letter."

"Well, what happened?"

"He wrote back, thanking me for updating him on my life. He enclosed a number and wants me to call him back."

"Well, are you?"

"Randy wants to. He wants to call this afternoon. Like when I get back home."

"So, that's good news, right?" Regina adds, crinkling her forehead as if she has no idea where this conversation is going.

Back when we were teenagers and Karen's folks split up, Karen's dad vowed never to speak to her again if she chose to continue seeing that nigger, referring to Randy. Karen was hurt and spent a few days sulking and calling him names. Her dad hadn't been around most of her life anyway, so she finally concluded that she could do without him as an adult. And she did fine for a few years, until her mother died. Her mother had been silently supportive, but when she died and Karen lost her one link to family, the void of not having her dad overwhelmed her. Over the years, we spent countless "girls' nights out" talking about what she should do, only to end up doing nothing. But cancer had shone things in a whole new light. Karen had reached out, with no idea what kind of response she would get.

"They are whispering about us."

"Yeah, I guess we look a little strange all crammed in this stall."

The three of us do the group hug thing and ignore the spectators' rude comments.

"Only true friends would shut themselves in a bathroom stall with you and hug and cry. Thanks, guys."

We hug some more before coming out acting just like it's completely normal for three women to exit a tiny bathroom stall. Two ladies at the sink avoid eye contact. Another, coming out of one of the other stalls, takes a quick look at all three of us, shakes her head, and walks out the door.

"Bitch didn't even wash her nasty-ass hands, and got the nerve to look at us down her uppity nose," Regina says as we watch the other ladies drying their hands and bolting for the door.

When we get back to our seats, Butt Cheek is busy trying to refill water glasses that aren't empty. We take our seats, watching Cheek taking an order at the table beside us, scribble something on a notepad, and scamper off with her shorty shorts riding up into her tight little ass. We all laugh at the sight and start the bets on whether or not she is wearing underwear.

37

"So, are you bringing someone to the banquet tonight?" Karen says, almost causing both Regina and me to choke.

We had avoided it the first time when Karen ran out crying, but there it was again. This time we would not be able to avoid it. I gently place my fork down beside the salad bowl and wait; watching the gloves come off, ready to referee. Regina's relationships have been a sore subject between the two of them forever. I wonder how bad it will get this time, since the date is now a woman.

"You just had to go there, didn't you, miss goody two shoes?"

"I asked a simple question. Are you bringing a date or not? Yes or no, it's not brain surgery, Regina."

I listen as the two of them go back and forth about the question. The salad isn't very good and the tuna needs more mayonnaise, so I make myself content to simply take in every word of this fight. I tilt my head back to the side and go back and forth like a spectator at a tennis match.

"I just think you're jumping the gun. Reginald's proposal scared you and all of a sudden you're gay, writing all men off. I just think you're not dealing with the real issue."

"And why don't you tell me what the real issue is, Karen? Please tell me what Mrs. Perfect has to say about my situation."

"Yeah, I'm perfect; my sisters won't have anything to do with me, my mom died of cancer and never got to see me graduate from college, I had cancer, and my dad, well, who knows what's gonna happen with that. I'm not perfect, but I'm not copping out, either."

"You're so sure I'm copping out. Jumping the gun as you put it. Why do you even get an opinion? This is my life," Regina yells, getting a few glances from other restaurant patrons.

Hooters isn't a quiet place at lunchtime, but an argument of this magnitude is more than the blaring Top Forty radio station tunes can cover.

"Because I care, dammit. Because I care, that's why," Karen says, choking back tears.

I hand her a tissue and wait for the battle to start up again. This is how it works with these two. They fight like cats and dogs. It's the only way they get through things. Reginald had proposed to Regina, scared the daylights out of her, and made her face her horrible past. Her fear of commitment. After steering clear of Karen for months, she announced that she was taking on an alternative lifestyle. Karen blew a fuse. I didn't take it too seriously, assuming it was just another one of her things. She'd miss getting poked by the real thing and drop the whole lesbian crap. But after nine months, she is still holding to her new lifestyle.

"So if you care so much, then why can't you just accept this? Why?"

Butt Cheek must've heard some of the conversation because she is spending most of her time on the other side of the room. I finally get her attention and hold my water glass in the air, signaling that I need a refill. She hurries over with the water pitcher, not even flinching as her shorts fully ascend into her butt crack. I am glad the food isn't good. I'd have certainly lost my appetite just imagining how she'd have to pry the fabric from between the two tanned slabs of flesh.

"I'm bringing someone tonight. And if you really care about me, you'll drop this. I'm the first to admit I have relationship problems and scars from my troubled childhood, but dammit, who doesn't? This is where I am now; I'd appreciate having you on my side, not against me."

"I'm sorry. I just don't want to see you get hurt."

"Well, fighting with you hurts. So, you're the one hurting me now," Regina confesses, wiping her tears with the tiny napkin displaying the Hooter owl eyes.

Karen sits motionless for a few seconds. I assume she is letting Regina's words sink in. She reaches over and grabs Regina's hand and they both start giggling to signal truce. That's how it ends. I figure I've missed something although my eyes have been glued to the two of them since Karen first asked if she was bringing a date.

"Well, she'd better not be ugly or too pretty. That's all I got to say." I add my two cents' worth, grab the check, and head to the cash register to pay.

Regina volunteers to give Karen a ride home so I can stop by the shop before going home to get dressed for my big night. We exit Hooters, leaving Butt Cheek and a few confused patrons behind. I wave goodbye as I head toward the parking garage to get my car. I watch the two women walk off chatting like they haven't just been ripping at each other's soul. The only word that comes to mind is support. We always support each other. We don't always want to and we usually fight good and hard about it, but when the rubber meets the road, we got each other's back. Those two fools are part of the reason I have my own business.

Since I'm a chronic workaholic and the boys are going straight to Mama's after school, I decide to swing by Hole In One before going home to dress for the banquet. There is nothing in particular I need to do at the shop. I hired highly motivated, intelligent people to run the business, but sometimes I like to stop by and just look at it. The name on the front of the building, the workers and customers inside. All buzzing around the best shoes and handbags in the area. Hole In One pulls in the unique golfing community, but it isn't too rare to find nongolfers stopping by just to see and enjoy the goodies.

When I walk into the store, there are three women shopping. The store manager and sales clerk that work the day shift are attending to their needs. They all look at me when I walk in. Then they all smile. By now, word has spread that a black woman owns the store, and I no longer get the startled looks when I walk into my own business establishment. I shake my head to let them know that I don't want anything in particular. They go back to waiting on the ladies who are actually getting Father's Day gifts for the special men in their lives. My mind tosses a quick shot of Tyrese Basnight, and then a smile creeps across my face. This date has to go better than the one a year ago.

I spend no more than thirty minutes in the store before I wave goodbye. The same customers are done shopping and now greedily shoving the fresh pastries and sandwiches into their mouths.

"Skipped lunch," one lady proclaims.

"Help yourself," I whisper and push through the front door to greet the remainder of a warm spring day.

I stand in front of the shop pretending to be looking down the street, but instead my eyes are glued to the sign above the shop. Jessi's Hole In One in dark, bold black letters, with a picture of a golf bag and a pair of golf shoes off to the left. The average passerby would think I am crazy or slightly self-absorbed, but those who know me would know I am just an extremely grateful woman.

All my gratefulness and thankfulness washes off my face as I see Reverend Lemuel Harris, Pastor of the New Deliverance Church, walking toward me. Since I have never seen the reverend in the area before, I assume the worst. He is coming after me. To bring me back to the church.

"Sister Andrews, I been hoping to run into you here," he says, slightly out of breath.

I notice that he's put on a pound of two, and I stick my chest out bolder since I have lost more than thirty.

"It's good to see you too. Didn't know you frequented Ponte Vedra, Reverend," I say, hoping to catch him in a lie.

"I don't. Just came here looking for you. Your mama told me about the stores, the one downtown and this one. Said I'd likely find you here."

I smile and make a mental note to thank Mama.

"Nice day, isn't it," he adds, looking toward the sky and then at the store.

"Yes it is, Reverend. I hate to be rude, but I have an engagement tonight and I really must be going."

"I don't mean to hold you, Jessi." He pauses, again looking back toward the building, his eyes lingering on a palm tree that is part of the landscaping of the shop.

"Yes sir," I say, trying to watch my manners since Mama still goes to the church and respects the man. And plus I don't want to act ugly right in front of my own shop.

"You know, there's an interesting fact about palm trees," he says and pauses as if for dramatic effect.

I look at the same tree he was staring at, hoping the palm tree obsession will end soon.

"Palm trees like that one can take a whole lot of pressure. Hurricanes and strong winds and storms like the ones we get here in Florida all the time. And if you see them during the storm, they bend, and bend, almost touch the ground," he adds and pauses again.

"But they never break. They bend, Jessi, but they don't break."

I keep my eyes glued to the tree, although I know the Reverend is looking at me. His words are strong and powerful, and I can't bear to look away from the tree.

"And you know something? After the storm is over, the tree is actually taller," he laughs. "Yep, believe it or not, it grows," he finishes, and touches me on the shoulder before walking away.

Just like that, standing right in front of my successful golf shop, Reverend Lemuel Harris has preached a sermon. A private one, just for Jessi Andrews.

The ladies finally come out of the shop and I wipe tears from my cheeks realizing how insane I look, still standing in front of the shop, staring at a palm tree, crying. The ladies are laughing and munching as they approach me.

"I just want to say that this is a great store. And not just because you have the best shoes and bags, but it's the atmosphere too. Warm and welcoming, like visiting a friend," one lady says, as the other nods and chimes in.

"Yes Ms. Andrews, you really have something here."

"That's what my mother says," I offer, not sure what else to say.

"Well, your mother is right, dear. Keep up the good work. And we'll definitely be coming back here."

38

When I get home, I don't bother to check the machine or thumb through the mail, or turn on the television for a quick news update. My mind is lingering back on everything, so I decide that I need something more than a shower. I pour myself a glass of wine and run a bath.

My thoughts are of Ty Basnight as I undress to take a good long hot soak. I wrap my hair in a silk scarf to make sure it doesn't get wet in the bath. Glancing in the mirror I wink at the lady looking back. Not too slim, curves in all the right places. I turn around to get a look at the caboose. That too is tight and firm, but still large enough to fill out a pair of Gucci's. The working out has served me well, but not just because of the weight loss, but the energy boost. It would have been tough to run my own business the way I felt a year ago. Low self-esteem and poor eating habits had battled for every waking moment of my life. Now my days consist of trying to figure out how to squeeze a little bit more work into my daylight hours and a little bit more play into my nights.

The bear-claw-shaped Jacuzzi tub is filled, so I turn on the jets and give it the quick toe test.

"Perfect," I say as I slide into the water, settle against one of the jets and let my heart and soul bathe in the serene, quiet place of peace. His face pops into my head again and I can't control the smile that slides across my lips as I grab the glass of wine from the side of the tub. A jazz tune is playing softly in the background. So soft in fact, I have to almost strain to hear it. I play my music soft to let it seep into my subconscious while my mind lingers and plays with other things. Mr. North Carolina, I think, trying to picture Ty at home getting ready for a date with me. He is all I can think about as I lay in the lukewarm bath water watching the bubbles slowly disappear and my naked body pierce through. I relax and soak until all the hot has seeped out of my hot bath. The phone rings just as I am about to nudge the lever with my big toe to let the water out.

"Hello . . ."

"Hey Jess, I know you're getting ready because its 6:00, but I have . . ."

"Oh my God, I lost track of time. I gotta go. I haven't started dressing yet. Ty will be here any minute."

"But Jess, I have a problem, and who the hell is Ty?"

Regina is in crisis mode, as if I am not shriveling up like a prune in cool bathwater when I should be pulling an evening gown over my head and doing something with my hair.

"Yes, Regina, what is it?"

"How do I introduce her? I mean what do I call her?"

"What's her damn name? That's what you call her."

"No I mean, who do I say she is. Do I say, everyone this is Tiffany, my girlfriend, or lover, or friend . . . what do I call her?"

"I don't know. What is protocol?"

"There's no damn manual for this, you know. You don't go to the lesbian recruit station and get briefed on how to handle public functions. You gotta help me."

"Ask her. She's been at it longer than you, right? She probably knows what you should call her."

"That's good, I'll do that. You're a lifesaver. Thanks, and who the hell is Ty?"

"I met him at the bank this morning. He's my date."

"Damn, girl. Don't waste no time, do you? Got yo' business going and now you just see what you want and go get it."

"Bye, Regina."

"I'll see you there, girl, and this Ty fool better be all that."

I hope you see me there, I think, as I hit the power button on the phone, jump over the edge of the tub and grab a towel. Before I can get myself dried off good, the doorbell rings. It is Ty. Why the hell is he so early? I don't have time for this. What in the world am I gonna do with my hair, I scream as I walk by the bathroom mirror and notice that my hair had gotten wet in the bathtub.

I wrap the towel around my still dripping body and run to the door to let Ty in. He can make himself at home while I finish dressing. I open the door expecting to grab Ty, yank him inside, and run back to my bedroom to get dressed. But when I open the door, I get the shock of my life.

"Wow, now that's the way you answer the door. You shoulda come to the door like this when we were married."

"Derrick, what the hell?" I yell, watching this common fool licking his lips, eyes running up and down my almost naked wet body.

I let him in against my better judgment. I don't want him to think that letting him into my home is in any way letting him into my life, or that he even matters one way or another. He shuts the door behind him but stays close to it. I stand there with my arms folded, looking at him with piercing eyes.

"Damn baby, what I wouldn't do to switch places with that towel."

"Did you come here for any reason in particular?"

"As a matter of fact I did, but can we sit down for a minute?"

"No we cannot. I'm on my way out, running late, and growing very impatient with this scene."

"Okay, I'll get to the point," he says shuffling from one foot to the other.

"My business went under. It's been struggling for some time now, but I just decided to get out before I lost everything. And Minnie, well, she didn't seem to feel like supporting a brother until he could get on his feet again."

"And I'm supposed to care about this . . ."

"No, I just wanted to let you know I'm leaving town. Trying

to line up a gig in Baltimore. I got a boy up there who got connections in the studio. I'm gonna try my dream, you know, the jazz thing," he adds, looking around the upscale apartment.

I tighten my towel, wishing I'd never opened the door.

"Okay, have a good trip," I say pushing past him to open the door.

"Hold up, hold up. So it's like that," he adds, shaking his big head. "Well, I'm really here cause I heard your store is doing pretty good and I kinda need a little something to help me get going up the road. Just a loan, and looking at this place, you could definitely spare a grand, for old times' sake."

I watch Derrick closely as he runs his game. I wonder what I ever saw in him. He isn't that handsome. His gut has jumped back over his belt and he has the nerve to be standing in my home begging me for money to move on with his life. Some things never change. When I reach to open the door to let Derrick out, I get yet another surprise.

"It looks like I caught you in the middle of something," Ty says as he steps into the apartment surveying me in a towel and Derrick in a gangsta pose with his arms crossed up around his chest.

"Hi Tyrese, come on in," I say giving him a quick peck on the cheek, and taking the bouquet of flowers from his hand.

It's all out there. I am standing in front of two men wearing only a towel, running late for a banquet to honor my accomplishments. My eyes bounce between the two men as I smirk at the irony. Men, I think as I take the bull by the horns.

"This fool is my ex-husband. He stopped by to let me know he's still as ignorant and no-good as ever. He lost his used-car business, the same business where I found him cheating on me, and now he needs some of my hard-earned money to move his no-account ass up north."

Ty looks at me and then back at Derrick, who has dropped his hands down by his side by the time I finish the introductions.

"Oh, so it's like that. Gonna throw your new man all up in my face."

"You had the nerve to screw your woman right in front of my face."

"Listen Jessi, if he's bothering you, I could . . ."

"I'm a big girl, Ty, I can handle this one myself, but thanks for the offer," I say, turning my attention back to Derrick.

"Get out of my house, Derrick Andrews, and please forget where I live and that you ever knew me, and I'll do likewise."

I open the door, watch as Derrick gives Ty evil eyes and vice versa. They look like two pit bulls matched against each other in battle. I shake my head in disgust as Derrick finally gets far enough out the door for me to slam it.

"Make yourself at home, I've got to dress," I say to Ty as I readjust my towel and silk headscarf and make my way to the bedroom. A new feeling has replaced the nagging in the pit of my stomach. I slide my feet across the plush carpet in my bedroom, part of the new Liz Claiborne line. I like her clothes and perfume, so I decided the carpet can't be half bad. I open the double doors to the closet and pull out the J. Rouse evening gown. I let the towel drop and slide the dress over my head. I let it shimmy to the floor and walk to the full-length mirror to take a look.

"A good two months' salary, and worth every penny."

I have spent too many years of my life only dreaming about the red chiffon evening slip dress. The two layers of dreamy fabric move with my body as if they were one. I add a pair of pearls and pull out the matching droplet earrings, slide them onto my ears and continue to slowly take in the sight that is forming before my eyes. My mind is so far from the man standing in my living room. At this point all that matters is what is before my eyes.

My short, sassy haircut is perfect for a time like this. I yank off the silk scarf and run my fingers through it to fluff the parts that had been flattened while I was in the tub. In the bathroom mirror I peer into eyes that need no mascara or liner. A light dusting of powder and the once-over with a new shade of lipstick I'd picked up. I almost left the tube in the store since it looked more like a clear gloss than lip color. I rub it across the bottom and then the top lip. Rubbing them together and then giving myself a kiss, it is simply perfect. A little gloss to accentuate the natural tone of my lips. Tonight is all about natural beauty and natural talent.

Since there was so much drama when Ty first arrived, I hadn't gotten a chance to check him out. I walk back into the living room to start with my preparations for leaving the house: Turn on a light over the stove in the kitchen, a lamp in the living room, set the alarm, etc. I glance at him sitting nervously on my couch probably wondering what the hell he's gotten himself into. He is wearing a black tuxedo with tails. Black bow tie hugging him like a long-lost relative. I hadn't expected him to be completely formal, but I am glad he went all out. I'm worth it.

He stands up and opens the door without once asking about what happened earlier. He compliments my gown, jewelry, perfume, and even the lipstick. His points are adding up quickly, but the jury is still out, that is until we walk out of my apartment to the white super-stretch limousine. The driver meets me at the bottom of the steps with extended hand and ushers me to the back door. I look back and give Ty a smile and wink to show my appreciation as I step into the car whose interior is covered in plush blue velvet and bronze-plated fixtures. I scoot and squirm to get comfortable in the seat as I watch a handsome and intelligent man scoot in by my side.

"Hope it's not too much. The ladies at the bank got to talking about you after you left. Said you sell the best shoes in town, expensive though. I told myself a lady like that deserves a little something more than my Honda Accord."

"Your Honda would have been just fine," I lie, as he pops open a bottle of champagne.

"Kind of exciting, back there at your house. You see him often?"

"I hadn't seen him in almost a year. Hadn't planned to see him at all."

"You handled it nicely, mighty nice matter of fact."

I could listen to that southern talk all night, but after a half glass of champagne we are there. The Jackson Building downtown, right on the water. The limo pulls around the oval-shaped driveway in front of the building. I can see Karen and Randy chatting with Regina and a girl who at first glance is stunning.

The driver opens the door and Ty gets out first. I pause and let him straighten his jacket and extend his hand. I make my grand exit and by the time I gracefully get out and stand erect beside Ty, the clapping starts. Karen and Randy, Regina, her friend, and several of the members of the CEO Roundtable that have just arrived. I throw up my hand to get them to stop, knowing full well I am loving every minute of it. The limousine, the fine man at my side, my friends applauding my entrance. It feels good, damn good, and I deserve it, so I drop my hand and nod my head modestly.

The banquet hall is full of important people in glittering gowns and tailored suits. An usherette directs us to a large, round table toward the front. Our names are written in on dinner cards shaped like colorful high-heel pumps. There is even a silver pump with Ty's name on it. How did they know he was coming? I wonder briefly before I am interrupted by a hand on my shoulder. I spin around like a lady should wearing a J. Rouse, elegantly acknowledging whoever wanted my attention.

"This is my friend, Tiffany," Regina announces.

She went with friend. It sounds okay. She looks like a Tiffany; petite and even prettier than I had first thought when I saw them outside. She is wearing a coral mesh halter dress, embellished with swirls of cracked ice glitter. She stands beside Regina sparkling, looking like she will break into pieces if Regina speaks too loudly. And her shoes are Weitzman. I know them on sight. I like her.

"It's nice to meet you, Tiffany, so glad you could join us."

Regina and Tiffany leave for the ladies' room. Regina is doing her thing too, in her black and gold chiffon number. Leaving nothing to the imagination, just as Regina would want it. When the light hits it just right, you can see the thong panties underneath. We watch them walk off before anyone makes a comment.

"Well, I think she's hot," Randy says, breaking the silence.

Karen slaps him on the back and we all laugh.

"And I see you got bold, Mrs. St. Clair. Strapless is daring. Not trying to show off those nipples are you?" I lean in and whisper in her ear.

Just as Karen and I finish teasing each other, in walks Mama and two handsome young men. I had told her that the boys' Sunday suits were fine, but they too are dressed in formal wear.

"Well, don't you two just steal my heart," I say reaching for both of them.

They pull away slightly. They're getting to that age where it's not cool to let your mother hug and kiss you in public, but they allow it since it's my big night.

"Tyrese, these are my sons Joshua and Jared. Guys, this is Mr. Basnight."

The boys politely shake hands with Ty, and then it's time for Mama.

"Mr. Basnight, I am Jessi's mother, Emma Cannon. It's a pleasure to meet you," she says as we all wait for something more.

She has a smirk on her face, and I can't put my finger on it, but I think she's trying to be mischievous.

"Pleasure to meet you, Mrs. Cannon. I'm honored to be part of this event tonight. Just met your daughter today at the bank," he says, his voice trembling as he can't seem to keep his lips from moving.

"Well, relax and enjoy yourself, son. Just remember this young lady, Jessi, she's the real thing, and I expect her to be treated like it."

Ty nods and looks at the rest of us to gauge her statement. We all laugh so that he can breathe again. He wipes sweat from his brow just as Regina and Tiffany are coming out of the ladies' room. A couple of swanky businessmen stop them at the door and start their obvious come-on lines. We all giggle at the sight. All except Ty, who hasn't been let in on the joke yet.

"They're gay, man," Randy whispers to Ty, so the boys can't hear him.

Ty nods and looks again toward the door where the two are standing.

"Oh, I see. Boy, you all sure know how to keep it interesting. I walk in on you half naked with your ex," he says pointing toward me, "and now you tell me those two pretty women are together. Wow, and the night ain't even started yet," he ends.

We all laugh and take our seats as the band starts a tune and the latecomers shift around in the dim light trying to find their names on a table. Regina and Tiffany return and take their seats without any awkward stares from anyone at the table. I am just about to ponder what it might feel like to be escorted someplace by a woman, when my name is called.

After two awards for business excellence and one for businesswoman of the year, I let the tears roll. The applause rings in my head as Ty stands to help me with my seat. I look around and they are all standing. Not just my guests, everyone in the place. All standing and clapping as I sit back down. Through tear-stained eyes I survey the room, not trying to see faces but wanting to permanently store this scene in my memory bank. Men and women in all shades and shapes, clapping and cheering. Karen crying equally as hard; part from hormones and part from sheer joy. Randy with one arm around her and the other swinging violently in the air, his hand balled into a fist. He is shouting something. Regina, with both hands cupped around her mouth to control the sound of the sobs. She hates crying in public. She always says people look so unattractive when they cry. Mouth torn open, eyes squinted, cheeks bunched as if in pain. It is a pretty sight to me. Mama trying to be dignified sits with her tissue dabbing her eyes occasionally. She's nodding her head up and down, like she's saying yes to someone across the room. And the boys are both looking around the room just as I am. They seem shocked that everyone is yelling and hooting for their mother. A look of pride stretches across their faces. Tiffany and Ty both oblivious to it all, but taking in everything. The newcomers to the group, we hope.

As the applause dies down and people start to take their seats, I think back to the nagging that had attacked me that day almost three years ago. That same nagging that started my day today. I had been so afraid of it. Something was about to happen. I smile, realizing that after all I've been through, I'm not afraid of that feeling anymore. Something is always happening; it's called life, and I for one am glad to have it. It sure as heck beats the alternative.

AFTER THE STORM

CASSANDRA DARDEN BELL

ABOUT THIS GUIDE

The questions and discussion topics that follow are intended to enhance your group's reading of AFTER THE STORM by Cassandra Darden Bell. We hope the novel provided an enjoyable read for all your members.

1. Jessi catches her husband in the act with another woman. Although she had suspected his infidelity in the past, there was no denying what she saw; however, based on her own self-esteem issues, do you think she would have left Derrick for good had he not made this decision for her?

2. In what ways has Jessi's relationship with her mother contributed to her self-esteem issues?

3. In the beginning, Jessi spoke of a church relationship that seemed at the cornerstone of her relationship with Derrick. After her marriage ends, she doesn't go back to the church. Why do you think she runs away from this institution at her greatest time of need?

4. Jessi's best friends, Karen and Regina, are as different as night and day. What role did each of them play in Jessi's dealing with and triumphing over adversity?

5. Jessi's friends take her on the vacation of a lifetime. After she realizes the trip is nothing like what she had imagined, what are some of the key points of revelation she faces while roughing it in the frozen tundra?

6. Karen's breast cancer struggle obviously affected everyone close to her. In what way did this fight aid Jessi in her own transformation?

7. Jessi's relationship with her mother comes to a head. Discuss the turning point and what changes take place in the two women.

8. We are aware of Jessi's love of shoes and handbags at the onset of the story. As life deals her a staggering blow, she leans on what seems like an overpriced hobby for answers to the future. Discuss the idea of using your own natural talents and skills to take your life in a new and prosperous direction.

9. Jessi's success as an entrepreneur is phenomenal, but do you think she would have seen this same level of success

had her world not been tossed upside down by the loss of her marriage? Also, discuss Jessi's two confrontations with Derrick after she's reinvented herself.

10. At the closing banquet, Jessi is sitting around the table with the key players in her new life. Discuss what you think will happen with these players: Karen and Randy, Regina and her new love interest, Jessi and her mother, and Jessi and the new man in her life.